The Case of the Three Arrests

The Case of the Three Arrests

From the Case Files of Attorney Daniel Marcos

Jeffery Sealing

iUniverse LLC
Bloomington

The Case of the Three Arrests
From the Case Files of Attorney Daniel Marcos

iUniverse books may be ordered through booksellers or by contacting:

iUniverse LLC
1663 Liberty Drive
Bloomington, IN 47403
www.iuniverse.com
1-800-Authors (1-800-288-4677)

Because of the dynamic nature of the Internet, any web addresses or links contained in this book may have changed since publication and may no longer be valid. The views expressed in this work are solely those of the author and do not necessarily reflect the views of the publisher, and the publisher hereby disclaims any responsibility for them.

Any people depicted in stock imagery provided by Thinkstock are models, and such images are being used for illustrative purposes only.
Certain stock imagery © Thinkstock.

ISBN: 978-1-4917-1518-5 (sc)
ISBN: 978-1-4917-1519-2 (e)

Printed in the United States of America.

iUniverse rev. date: 11/27/2013

Don't ever give up thinking that you cannot change the world in which you live. A warrior is someone who not only fights for the homeland, but also must defend those who cannot, or are powerless to, defend themselves. Jeffery Sealing

To Karena and Bill at the Blue Moon Akita Rescue in Aurora, Colorado, for letting us adopt Ricky. Ricky is a rescue Akita; check them out at www.bluemoonakitarescue.com.

Acknowledgement: I would like to say thank you to the wonderful people of the Colorado Bar Association for providing me the necessary background information for this book. Perhaps this issue will finally come to pass one day long after I am gone. To all of those who are waiting, be patient, justice will be served.

To Hope Painter, retired English teacher, for providing the editing services on this, my last book.

DISCLAIMER: This fictional case is based on Colorado Revised Statutes. Therefore, Colorado Law Procedures, Title 16 and the Criminal Code, Title 18 are mentioned or referenced for legal definitions only. Always consult an attorney in all legal cases. The town of Ironton is real, but no longer exists. The town, for the purposes of this book, was placed outside of Silverton, Colorado, for security reasons due to the September 11, 2001 terrorist attacks. Other towns mentioned are real as they are in the counties mentioned.

Preamble to the United States Constitution:
"We the People of the United States, in Order to form a more perfect Union, establish Justice, insure domestic Tranquility, provide for the common defense, promote the general Welfare, and secure the Blessings of Liberty to ourselves and our Posterity, do ordain and establish this Constitution for the United States of America."

Preamble to the Constitution for the State of Colorado:
"**We, the people of Colorado**, with profound reverence for the Supreme Ruler of the Universe, in order to form a more independent and perfect government; establish justice; insure tranquility; provide for the common defense; promote the general welfare and secure the blessings of liberty to ourselves and our posterity, do ordain and establish this constitution for the "State of Colorado"."

Article IV, Clause I United States Constitution:
"Full Faith and Credit shall be given in each State to the public Acts, Records, and judicial Proceedings of every other State. And the Congress may by general Laws prescribe the Manner in which such Acts, Records and Proceedings shall be proved, and the Effect thereof."

I pledge allegiance to the Flag
of the United States of America,
and to the Republic for which it stands:
one Nation under God, indivisible,
With Liberty **and Justice for all.**

AMENDMENT V

No person shall be held to answer for a capital, or otherwise infamous crime, unless on a presentment or indictment of a Grand Jury, except in cases arising in the land or naval forces, or in the Militia, when in actual service in time of War or public danger; nor shall any person be subject for the same offence to be twice put in jeopardy of life or limb; **nor shall be compelled in any criminal case to be a witness against himself**, nor be deprived of life, liberty, or property, without due process of law; nor shall private property be taken for public use, without just compensation.

Amendment 14

1. All persons born or naturalized in the United States, and subject to the jurisdiction thereof, are citizens of the United States and of the State wherein they reside. **No State shall make or enforce any law which shall abridge the privileges or immunities of citizens of the United States**; nor shall any State deprive any person of life, liberty, or property, without due process of law; **nor deny to any person within its jurisdiction the equal protection of the laws.**

42 U.S.C. 1983

Section 1983 of Title 42 of the United States Code provides, in part:

§ 1983. Civil action for deprivation of rights

"Every person who, under color of any statute, ordinance, regulation, custom, or usage, of any State or Territory or the District of Columbia, subjects, or causes to be subjected, any citizen of the United States or other person within the jurisdiction thereof to the deprivation of any rights, privileges, or immunities secured by the Constitution and laws, shall be liable to the party injured in an action at law, suit in equity, or other proper proceeding for redress, . . ."

Article II, Section 29, Colorado State Constitution

Equality of rights under the law shall not be denied or abridged by the state of Colorado or any of its political subdivisions on account of sex.

I Corinthians 13: 4-7

"Love is very patient and kind, never jealous or envious, never boastful or proud. Never haughty or selfish or rude, love doesn't demand its own way. It's not irritable or touchy. It doesn't hold grudges and will hardly even notice when others do it wrong. It's never glad about injustice, but rejoices whenever truth wins out. If you love someone, you will be loyal to him no matter what the cost. You will always believe him, always expect the best of him and always stand your ground in defending him."

Nowhere does it say love sees someone's height, weight, ethnicity or sexual orientation/preference. You will find no where it says that you have to be a doctor, lawyer, judge, etc., to receive love. Society has placed all sorts of "conditions" on unconditional love and unconditional acceptance. If you are truly human or humanoid, besides unconditional acceptance and unconditional love, you must also possess the quality of the willingness of self-sacrifice.

John 15: 13

"I demand that you love each other as much as I love you and here is how to measure it—the greatest love is shown when a person lays down his life for his friends."

Miscegenation

A mixture of the races, especially in the context of marriage and procreation.

An *ex post facto* law (from the Latin for "from after the action") or retroactive law is a law that retroactively changes the legal consequences (or status) of actions committed or relationships that existed prior to the enactment of the law.

Chief Justice John Marshall

"It is a proposition too plain to be contested, that the constitution controls any legislative act repugnant to it . . . ." *Marbury v. Madison*, 5 U.S. (1 Cranch) 137, 177, 2 L. Ed. 60, 73 (1803).

Justice Oliver Wendell Holmes poignantly said, "It is revolting to have no better reason for a rule of law than that so it was laid down in the time of Henry IV. It is still more revolting if the grounds upon which it was laid down have vanished long since, and the rule simply persists from blind imitation of the past."

Article I, Section 10, Clause 1, United States Constitution:

No State shall enter into any Treaty, Alliance, or Confederation; grant Letters of Marque and Reprisal; coin Money; emit Bills of Credit; make any Thing but gold and silver Coin a Tender in Payment of Debts; pass any Bill of Attainder, ex post facto Law, or Law impairing the Obligation of Contracts, or grant any Title of Nobility.

CHAPTER 1

It was beginning to rain on the window where Daniel stood, silently looking at the picture of Melanie Thompson. It was early morning, and Daniel had just finished stretching out prior to his workout. Today was going to be the eighth anniversary of Melanie's death and Chayton's eighth birthday. Daniel then realized that he would be turning fifty-two this year as well. He tried not to cry as he stared at her picture, but he couldn't help it. The pain was still there; although he did notice it had diminished over the years, just as Bill had said it would.

Since it was still very early in the morning, Daniel left Shilah in the bed. He then walked into the bathroom, closed the door and turned on the lights. As he looked into the mirror while shaving, he was able to get a good look at himself. His long, coal black straight hair flowed across his chest. Some of the hair had started to turn gray, but it didn't bother him. He finished shaving, rinsed his face and went downstairs to workout.

During the workout, he started reflecting on what had happened to him during the past four years: he had suffered some heavy losses. Jessica was a very happy wife with three kids who dearly loved Daniel. Since she seldom let him see them, he had learned the fine art of how to set up video conferencing on both his home and office computers.

Seth had left four years ago and married. Daniel couldn't understand why none of them had been invited to the wedding. He figured Seth had his reasons. Now, Todd was getting ready to leave the big house which made Daniel feel rather sad. He had also lost Mr. and Mrs. Thompson within a year of each other.

He finished working out and went back upstairs to take a shower. He then went to the kitchen to start making Chayton's birthday cake. While the oven was preheating, he turned on the TV in the kitchen to see what the weather was going to be like today in Durango and to check the news. He saw the female reporter talking about a breaking news story. The story dealt with a former client of his, so he turned up the volume to hear the report.

"This just in to the news room. Garth Wyles, convicted four years ago of killing a 6th judicial district prosecutor and the San Juan County, Colorado, Coroner, was executed this morning by lethal injection at the Terre Haute, Indiana federal correctional facility at 8:05 a.m. Eastern Standard Time." Daniel turned down the volume and put Chayton's birthday cake into the oven.

As the cake was baking, he mixed up the frosting and put the presents, which he had retrieved from the basement safe late the previous night, on the dining room table. He put the frosting into the refrigerator and closed the door. He thought he saw something moving to his left. Daniel turned around to see Chayton standing there in his pajamas and rubbing his eyes. Daniel smiled and spoke quietly to him as he picked him up.

"Good morning, Chayton, what does the birthday boy want?" he asked.

"Mommy back."

Those two words hit Daniel very hard; he almost started crying again.

"That makes two of us," said Daniel as he picked up Chayton.

That's when Daniel heard a voice from behind him.

"Make that three, Chayton," said Todd.

Daniel turned around to see Todd standing there in the doorway to the kitchen from the dining room. He was wearing his favorite bathrobe, the one Chayton had picked out for him one Christmas. Although Daniel thought it was the most hideous chartreuse green he had ever seen, he wasn't about to argue with Chayton. The smell of the baking cake was very noticeable now. After Daniel put Chayton down, he hugged Todd for a short time.

"What woke you up, Todd?" asked Daniel, suspicious of his early morning waking and wandering around.

"The smell of the angel food cake, Dad."

"Dad, did Seth send me a present?" asked Chayton.

"Yes, he did; let me get it for you," said Daniel as he squeezed past Todd and went to the basement. In a few seconds, he returned with the large brown box. He handed it to Chayton, who tore it open immediately. The box contained a stuffed toy dolphin, a couple of DVD's about dolphins and a nice letter. As Chayton headed for his room to watch the DVD's, he caught part of the conversation that Daniel and Todd were having.

"Dad, I mean Daniel, how come we weren't invited to Seth's wedding any way?" asked Todd.

"Yeah, Dad, why weren't we?" asked Chayton.

"I surmise that Seth believed we would not approve of his choice of a mate in life."

"Daniel, I'm not that stupid; no woman could be that ugly," said Todd.

Daniel looked directly at Todd before speaking.

"I'm not entirely certain he's married to a woman, Todd."

"Then who is he married to, a he-she?"

Daniel refocused his eyes sternly on Todd now.

"Where did you hear that disparaging term for those types of people?"

"From some of the guys at school, Daniel."

"Well, I don't want you to use that disparaging, pornographic term in my presence; do you understand me?"

"Yes, Dad, I understand."

"Dad, what's a he-she?"

"Great, thanks a lot for opening up that Pandora's box, Todd!" said Daniel as quietly as possible, but with heavy emphasis on Todd's name.

"Any time, Daniel!" replied Todd, with the emphasis on Daniel's name.

Thankfully for Daniel, the timer on the oven went off, and he pulled Chayton's cake out of the oven. He then carefully set it down on the countertop at the very back to cool properly. As Daniel opened the refrigerator to remove the frosting, he could feel

Chayton's stare from the kitchen table. Daniel turned around to see Chayton sitting in his chair at the kitchen table; Todd was also seated at the table. Daniel walked over to the table and sat down after setting the timer to tell him when the frosting was done.

"How in the hell do you explain what a hermaphrodite is to an eight year old?" thought Daniel.

"Dad, I asked you a question, and don't lie to me; I'm not that stupid," said Chayton.

"I never said you were stupid, Chayton; I'm just trying to figure out how to tell you so that you will understand."

"Why don't you tell him the truth; that's what you tell your clients, Dad."

"Good point, Todd. Chayton, the terms she-male, he-she or whatever other bad pornographic term is used, shouldn't be used in my presence or yours."

"Why?" asked Chayton.

"Those terms are considered to be degrading and dehumanizing to those people. Their legal definition is called hermaphrodite. There are a few people in this world called transgendered that have had what is called a gender reassignment surgery performed on them to turn them from either male to female or the other way around."

"A what?"

"The legal term is hermaphrodite."

"Have you ever been with one, Dad?" asked Todd.

"Funny you should mention that, Todd; I have been with two. One was an inmate at a correctional facility in Idaho, and the other one was at the U.S. Olympic Training Center in Colorado Springs. She was a track star representing her country when the International Olympic Committee found out about her during a random drug test. She was giving a motivational speech in 2009 at a lawyers conference I was attending."

"What's the word you used, Dad?"

"Her."

"Her."

"Maph."

"Matph."

"Ro."

"Row."

"Dite."

"Deete."

"Say the word all together now, Chayton."

"Hermapthrodeete."

"Close enough; keep practicing."

"Well, I'm still waiting."

"They are very rare and sometimes very secretative people because they know that they are different from everyone else around them. Generally, during the first three months of the baby's life in the womb, the body is waiting for either the boy code or the girl code to step across the line."

"Dad, I've already been taught that I am a boy because I have a penis, and that my friend Lucy, who sits next to me, is a girl because she has a vagina."

Daniel just rolled his eyes towards the ceiling.

"I'm glad to know that you understand the basics of boys and girls, Chayton. Now, what happens in these people is neither the boy code nor the girl code steps across the line, and the body develops both."

"You mean that they have both a penis and a vagina?" said Chayton, throwing his head back in amazement.

"Yes, but here in the United States, the parents of the child can tell the doctor whether they want a boy or a girl. They tell the doctor what their choice is, and the other sexual organ is removed. The insurance company gets billed for the whole thing."

"Wow!"

"Sometimes, such as in some third world countries, because of a term called socialized medicine, the parents cannot afford such a surgical procedure. Therefore the child grows up to develop both sexual organs and secondary characteristics. The inmate in Idaho had a very nice looking, muscular male body with a full set of breasts."

"They get teased, don't they, Dad?"

"Yes, that is one of the reasons why they're so quiet, shy and rare."

"Thanks, Dad, time to go watch my DVD."

"Don't forget your birthday party is at the Smith's this year at 10:15. Then we go to the pizza place for the rest of the party."

"I won't forget."

Chayton rushed out of the kitchen just as the timer went off. Daniel started putting the frosting on the cake and looked over at Todd.

"Well, did I pass the muster on that issue?"

"Yes, Dad, and do you happen to remember this Olympians' name?"

"Yes, I think her last name was Svoyia, and she was busted for allegedly using steroids. It turned out that she had internal testicles, but she still competed at the 2012 Olympics, taking home two gold medals for the 200 and 400 meter events and two silver medals for the 800 and 1600 meter events for her home country. Are you going to church services today?"

"Yes, with Kathy."

"Well, I think you had better try and get some more sleep then."

"Thanks, Dad," he said, going back upstairs to bed.

A few hours later and many changes of clothes and shoes, both Daniel and Chayton were happy with the color combination. Mrs. Smith helped out with all the presents. After locking up the front door, Daniel carefully packed the cake into the back of his car, and zipped up Chayton's jacket. They both stepped into the car and headed towards Durango.

"Dad, does Seth hate us?"

"No, of course not, he loves us all very much."

"Then why didn't he invite us to his wedding? I want to know why?"

"Chayton, I have reasonable suspicion that Seth believed we would not approve of his choice of a mate in life, as I mentioned earlier. No doubt, you have been taught about unconditional love and unconditional acceptance in your Sunday school classes."

"Yeah, the Creator loves us all, no matter what."

"Yes, that's right, and in this world you are free to marry whomever you want in most places. In some places, you are not allowed to marry someone if they are of the same sex; it is forbidden and in some of those places it is an executable offense for your love."

6

"Dad, you still haven't answered my question of why."

"Seth believed that we would scorn and ridicule him for his marriage."

Chayton was quiet for several minutes before turning around in his seat to face Daniel. He had a very serious look on his face.

"Is Seth married to another boy, then?"

"Well, that didn't take too long for him to figure it out," said Daniel to himself.

"I strongly suspect it because I had to do some paperwork for him when you were four. The legal term is same-sex marriage; these marriages are not valid or recognized in thirty-nine states and many foreign countries."

"Why?"

"There are people in this world who feel that those who have chosen a mate in life of the same-sex are inferior, non-committed persons who cannot fulfill all of the vows of a traditional marriage between a boy and a girl."

"That's wrong, Dad."

"Yes, it is, and the legal term is called discrimination. However, as long as the legislature or the voters enact Levitican type laws to enforce on everyone, the discrimination continues."

"Dad, why hate someone for who they love?"

"Chayton, there are some people in this world that don't fully understand what 1 Corinthians 13:4-7 really means. There are those who get a certain amount of enjoyment from treating others as inferior or second class citizens."

"Is there no hero for those types of people, Dad?"

"No, Chayton, there's no hero for them in thirty-nine states including this one."

"They need a hero, Dad."

"Can't argue with you there, Chayton."

"So, if Seth is married to another boy like you think he is, is his marriage good here?"

"No, the Colorado State Constitution was amended by the voters in 2006 with what was termed the Defense of Marriage Act or DOMA. Seth's alleged marriage is not valid or recognized in this state. In other words, he is a second class citizen, stripped of all the rights, privileges and immunities provided for by a traditional marriage and what you and I take for granted as U.S. citizens."

"Is that why he doesn't visit us?"

"Yes, I believe so."

"Why is there so much hate of people, Dad?"

"The hate that you refer to is directed at a group of people called the LGBTQ community. It stands for Lesbian, Gay, Bisexual, Transgender and Questioning or in some cases Queer."

"Are there any churches involved in the hate of these people?"

"A few are and, unfortunately, El Paso County and the cities of Colorado Springs and Monument have more churches headquartered there than any place else in the world. Some of my other lawyer friends refer to it as the religious stronghold of the United States."

"That's not right, Dad. I was taught in school that everyone is equal."

"Those were great words of an equally great speech, given by a man during a time when, while serving as the President of the United States, he was trying to keep the country together. This country was tearing itself apart over the words that our Founding Fathers put into the Preamble to the U.S. Constitution—'We the people . . .' and who they were talking about."

"The Civil War."

"That's correct, Chayton. During that time, a person's skin color or ethnicity determined how much value he had or how much of a tax the federal and state governments could charge for him."

"People were taxed back then?"

"Yes, your father here, because I am a Native American, or what the Constitution referred to as an Indian, was to be taxed as 3/5's of a person in accordance with what was then Article I, Section 2, Clause 3. But, when the 14th Amendment came along, and it was ratified by the required number of states at the time, that tax went away."

"So, not everyone is treated equally."

"No, but we have been working very hard since the Civil War to break down those hate barriers. In some cases there have been huge accomplishments, in others, huge disasters."

"I see."

Chayton was quiet for the rest of the trip. All the kids had fun at the pizza place in Durango. After everyone sang the happy birthday song to Chayton, the cake was completely gone in a matter of minutes. On the way home, Chayton fell asleep.

The next morning was the last day of school before the summer break started. Daniel went to his office early, and Todd drove Chayton to school. After school, while Daniel was in court, Todd picked up Chayton to take him home. They had a short conversation about Seth which ended badly with harsh words and threats being made against Seth. After dinner, Chayton said his prayers to the Creator, took a bath and went to bed.

They had arrived in Durango and checked into their hotel room. Cecilia Downs waited until after the door to the hotel room was shut, before looking over at her mate, Patricia Duffy-Downs. Cecilia went to get the rest of their luggage to bring back to the room. She then looked down at her cell phone for any sign of the other two parties in the appeals case. Since she saw no missed calls, no text messages, no emails and no voicemails, she tossed the cell phone down on the bed. One piece of luggage contained a copy of the court transcripts of their court cases in both electronic and hardcopy forms; Patricia looked up at Cecilia as she prepared to take a shower.

"Any word from the other two, yet?" asked Patricia.

"No, not yet," replied Cecilia.

"I don't think they're coming."

"Pat, they did get a much later start than we did; perhaps they haven't made it through the mountains far enough for a clear signal on their cell phones."

"Perhaps, but I think they chickened out."

"I don't think so; better get on with your shower."

Adam Smith looked over at his mate, Brian Good-Smith and then into the back seat of the large SUV they were driving. There was Tom Bell with his mate, John Delacruz-Bell, holding hands very tightly. The drive over both Monarch Pass and Red Mountain Pass was pretty scary. Since summer wasn't in full swing yet, there were patches of ice and snow-packed road surfaces. In some places on Red Mountain Pass near the top, the snow was higher than the

SUV. Brian looked down at his cell phone to finally see full signal strength instead of Analog Signal Only on the display.

"I'll make the call," he said, dialing Cecilia's cell phone number.

Cecilia's cell phone started ringing and after checking the Caller ID®, she answered.

"Glad to hear from you two," she said, feeling much more relieved now.

"Us as well; that drive over Red Mountain Pass at this time of the year is not for the faint of heart or claustrophobics."

"Yes, I can understand that; how about we meet you all for dinner at 7:00 in Durango? The restaurant is located at the corner of 5th Street and Railroad Avenue."

"Will do," he said, hanging up the phone and, using the GPS application on the phone, he punched in the address. According to the GPS, they were a little less than an hour away from the location.

At the dinner table, after drinks and appetizers had been served, Tom looked at Cecilia while eating.

"Are you sure we're doing the right thing this time? I think he's going to throw us out of his office just like all the others because he's afraid to defend our kind."

"I don't think so; he's a former public defender, a former prosecutor and now a very well-respected criminal defense attorney," said Cecilia.

"What makes you think he will take our appeals?" asked John.

"He's a family man, and he's been highly recommended by other lawyers here in Colorado as well as by the Colorado Bar Association's printout that we were given by Dianne."

"How are we going to get to his office?" asked Adam.

"I've purchased us all roundtrip tickets for passage on the Durango and Silverton Narrow Gauge Railroad. Tom, did you bring the transcripts of your court case?"

"Yes, Cecilia, it's in the back of the SUV."

"How about you, Adam?"

"Yes, it is in the back of the SUV as well."

"I still think he's going to throw us out of his office, just like all the others; he's a hater, too," said Patricia, chomping down very hard on a piece of her chicken from her chicken salad while the serving person, Jesse, poured the refills on their drinks.

"You won't find many haters in this town," he said, smiling.

"Really? Then do you know an attorney around this area by the name of Daniel Marcos?" asked Cecilia.

"Yeah I do, one of the best criminal defense attorneys' I've known. He would be the last person on this planet that I would put into the category of a bigot or racist."

"I wasn't going to say that," said Adam, rather defensively.

"But you were thinking it; enjoy your meals, folks," said Jesse as he left their table to tend to his other ones.

They paid for their dinners and went back to the hotel to get some semblance of sleep. Early the next morning, they ate breakfast at the hotel and left on the first train to Silverton. They shopped around Silverton and grabbed another cup of coffee each. As they drank their coffees, they walked up the road from Silverton to Ironton.

Cecilia was gripping the briefcase she had brought along very tightly. She gripped it so tightly that her right hand produced white knuckles; she was grinding her teeth slightly. They walked up the steps to Daniel's outer office and opened the double doors. Shilah came out from his inner office to the right of the door to greet them.

"Hello, folks, what can I do for you?" he asked, shaking everyone's hands. Adam, John, Brian and Tom all gawked at Shilah. Cecilia and Patricia looked him over then they looked at each other, giving each other the thumbs up.

"Nice body, dude," said Adam.

"Thanks, bro," replied Shilah who then turned to grab a tissue from the box that was sitting on the desk in front of the door; he handed the tissue to Adam.

"What's this for?" asked Adam, taking the tissue.

"To wipe the drool off of your chin," replied Shilah, smiling and winking at Adam. It was then that everyone started laughing and Cecilia felt that, this time, they had found the right person.

"I'm so sorry, Mr. Marcos," said John.

"I'm not Mr. Marcos; I'm his assistant criminal defense attorney, Shilah Haynes. Do you have an appointment with Mr. Marcos, today?"

"Yes, at 10:45, Mr. Haynes," said Cecilia, still clutching the briefcase handle with white knuckles.

"He'll be along in a few minutes. We have coffee, tea, water, and sodas to offer you," said Shilah, pointing to the coffee stand and the small refrigerator that was behind him as he walked back into his office.

They all sat down in the outer office chairs and small sofa. Daniel showed up a few minutes later. They all stood up, grabbed their mates' hands and smiled at Daniel. Daniel noticed he had six clients, four males and two females, waiting for him, and they were holding hands rather tightly. Everyone shook hands and Daniel noticed that the one female who had identified herself as Cecilia was clutching the briefcase handle tightly.

"Let me grab a cup of coffee and then we can talk in my inner office," said Daniel as he let them into his inner office and shut the door. Almost at once, everyone relaxed. Daniel returned, shut the door, and sat down at his desk.

CHAPTER 2

Daniel sipped his coffee and looked over at Cecilia and Patricia Duffy-Downs. Cecilia was a charming Asian-American woman, about five feet six inches tall and Daniel guessed weighed about one hundred ten pounds. She had long, flowing black hair that was very shiny. She kept it pulled back into a very tight ponytail. Patricia Duffy-Downs was an African-American woman, about five feet seven inches tall and Daniel guessed weighed about one hundred twenty pounds.

Next Daniel looked at Tom and John Delacruz-Bell. Tom and John were both handsome Latinos. Both were very tall at almost six feet and both had short, black hair and brown eyes. In fact, Daniel was wondering if they were twins as they looked so much alike. He guessed that they both weighed about one hundred fifty-five pounds. Daniel then looked at Adam and Brian Good-Smith. One was Caucasian, and the other had the looks of a Native American.

Daniel looked at Cecilia to see that she was more relaxed than earlier, and the color had returned to her right hand. She opened the briefcase and pulled out her status sheet on Daniel.

"What can I do for you people?" asked Daniel.

"We wish to appeal our convictions and you came highly recommended," said Cecilia.

"Were you all convicted of the same crime?"

"Yes, Mr. Marcos," said Adam.

"Please, you can call me Daniel. Brian, which nation are you affiliated with?"

"I'm a Lakota, Daniel; you don't miss much do you?" asked Brian, feeling a little nervous now.

"No, I try not to, especially when meeting clients for the first time. That's so I can tell if my client is lying to me; don't you agree, Tom?"

"Yes, Daniel," said Tom.

"Daniel, for someone your age, you have a really nice body," said John.

"Why, thank you, John, I appreciate that; were you all convicted in the same jurisdiction?"

"Yes, and by the same prosecutor," said Cecilia.

"Do you have copies of the court transcripts?"

Cecilia, Tom and Adam all nodded their heads up and down. They all handed Daniel the CD's of the court transcripts as well as hard copies. Daniel took them and set them down on the desktop.

"Cecilia, most people don't get as nervous as you were, a few minutes ago, until after I tell them what the bill is for my services; or were you certain that your briefcase was planning to escape at a moment's notice?" said Daniel, smiling, as everyone chuckled.

"Sorry, Daniel, every other attorney has tossed us out."

"That's a tragedy, Cecilia; did you twist the door knob off the doors to their offices?" asked Daniel, smiling.

Everyone chuckled again, even Cecilia, when she finally realized the humor of the situation.

"No, I don't think I did?" she said, now questioning herself.

"That's good. Has it been more than one hundred eighty days since your convictions?"

"No, about one hundred twenty," answered John, still staring at Daniel's chest and arms.

"Okay, where were you all convicted?"

"The 2nd judicial district," said Patricia.

"What crime or crimes were you all convicted of?"

"Domestic Violence, Daniel; we were at a private party with some friends and things went terribly wrong," said Patricia.

"Were there alcohol or drugs involved?"

"Alcohol, Daniel," said Brian.

"Okay, on the appeals process, do you want to file three separate appeals or do you want me to file as one party?"

"Could we file as one party, Daniel?" asked Cecilia.

"Sure and I will only charge one fee, which makes it easier for everyone to pay the fee. You mentioned earlier that I came highly recommended by other attorneys; do you have a list of those other attorneys?" asked Daniel, pulling out a pad of legal paper and a pen from out of his top, right desk drawer.

"The Colorado Bar Association Head, Rick Sanchez, suggested you because of your great work with high profile or high risk clients. I have a complete listing of the other attorneys we've seen in the last four months," she said, handing Daniel the list.

Daniel looked over the list which had twenty or so names. He recognized all of them as former judges, prosecutors or acquaintances of his. He saw at least one name that had been a Federal Circuit Court judge.

"I'm impressed, Cecilia, with this list of names. Were you aware that at least one of those attorneys is a former Colorado State Supreme Court associate justice?"

"I think she may have mentioned something like that to me while we were in her office in Meeker."

"So, Cecilia, what do you do for a living?"

"I'm an information brokerage specialist."

"I heard John here mention something about my age; what else do you know about me?"

Cecilia looked over her status sheet quickly.

"You have four kids, three that you are the legal guardian of, one that is yours. The woman who gave you those kids died shortly after giving birth to your son, Chayton. Is that name right?"

"Yes, please go on."

"You're a fifty-two year old, Native American who identifies with the Navajo nation. Since becoming a criminal defense attorney, you've only lost ten cases in fifteen years. You're also a former prosecutor and public defender."

"Well, I definitely think you have the right man for the appeals. So, is Cecilia going to be your spokesperson for the group?"

They all nodded their heads.

"Oh, and your son, Seth Thompson-Marcos, successfully sued his high school principal and won his case; did he retain you for that issue?"

"Yes, Seth was successful; do you happen to know what kind of a case it was?"

"A Title 42, United States Code, as amended, Section 1983, case number 17CV0001-KRJ in the 10th Federal Circuit Court."

"Very good, and, no, he didn't retain me for some unknown reason; he retained my associate, Attorney Mr. Haynes."

Daniel was quiet for a minute before speaking again.

"On what grounds do you wish me to appeal your convictions?" asked Daniel, ready to take notes.

"Daniel, although we all had public defenders, they allowed our rights to be exploited by the prosecution and the judge didn't seem to care," said John.

"Part of Colorado Revised Statutes, Title 18, Part 6, Article 800.3, Domestic Violence Statute, states that the prosecution has to prove two things. One, you have an intimate relationship of some kind and, two, a crime was committed," said Daniel, watching their reaction to his words.

"Daniel, in the eyes of Colorado law, our intimate relationships don't exist; therefore, how can we be convicted of a crime if the law says we don't exist?" asked Adam.

"But, you all did commit a crime; correct?"

"Yes, we beat the crap out of each other at that party over something really stupid someone else said," replied Brian.

"So, you all committed third degree assault then, I surmise?"

"Yes, something like that," replied Brian once again.

"Cecilia, do you and Patricia have any kids?" asked Daniel.

"Yes, we have four. They are nine, fourteen, sixteen, and seventeen; two from this relationship and the other two from previous relationships," said Patricia, proudly, as any mom would.

"Tom, do you and John have any kids?"

"Yes, we have two; they're eight and eleven; both boys," said Tom, proudly.

"What about you Adam and Brian, any kids?"

"One, and he's twelve," said Adam, beaming.

"I surmise, then, that your kids love you as much as you love them?" asked Daniel, looking at all of them individually this time.

"Yes," they all answered.

"Then, I will also surmise that you live in a family structure of some kind?"

"Yes, you could say that, Daniel," they all replied.

Daniel studied them for a few minutes before he realized who they were and why they had been sent to him.

"You all have same-sex marriages, don't you?" asked Daniel, already knowing the answer.

They all nodded their heads up and down; they all surmised that at this point Daniel was going to kick them out and that was the end of the line for their appeals. Instead, something else happened.

"You realize that when you entered this state, your marriages were nullified and voided in all respects, right?"

"Yes, our public defender said that our marriages, though legal and valid in fifteen states and several dozen foreign countries including the ones where we were married, are not valid or recognized here. He also said they were illegal," said Adam.

"Strangely enough, your marriages aren't illegal or prohibited. They're just not valid or recognized because the Colorado voters in 2006 passed the Defense of Marriage Act which modified the Colorado State Constitution. This doesn't make any sense to me or some of my colleagues. It seems that every other state with a voter approved Defense of Marriage Act initiative, has forced the legislature of that state to close off certain loopholes in the existing marriage laws."

"Are you going to toss us out, now that you know what we are?" asked Brian, nervously.

"No, I only throw out clients who lie to me or don't pay their bills that I send them."

Everyone chuckled once again and Daniel started to notice that his new clients were starting to relax a little.

"Thank you, Daniel," said Cecilia, much more relieved now.

"Anytime, Cecilia. Now, I do have a couple of questions to ask. Are the phone numbers and email addresses in the contact sections correct and up-to-date?"

They all nodded their heads up and down again.

"Can I, or an officer of the court, talk to your kids, neighbors or coworkers during the normal court day? And you're not going to tell them what to say to me; right?"

Again, they all nodded their heads.

"All right, I'll review the cases and get back to you as soon as I can. I have court this afternoon through about Thursday of next week. Can I call you on Friday the 19th?"

"Sure, our cell phone numbers are on the contact information page. We all have our cell phones on us at all times," said Cecilia.

"Good, please take a couple of my business cards. If you need to contact me for any reason, my email address is on there. Afterhours, weekends and holidays, the office number goes to my answering service. They will let me know who called."

"Thank you, Daniel," they all said, standing up and shaking hands as they left his office. Soon, they were on the return train trip to Durango, when Cecilia spoke to all of them.

"I am under the impression that he's going to take our cases," said Cecilia, relaxed and confident now.

"I hope so, for our sakes," said Adam.

"Adam, there's a lot more at stake here than you realize," said Tom.

"Like what?" asked Brian.

"If he takes on our appeals cases, he's not just representing us, he's representing the entire LGBTQ community within the State of Colorado," answered Patricia.

"Do you think he knows, yet?" asked John.

"No, but he's very smart and intuitive, he will figure it out," said Cecilia.

Rick Sanchez looked around his office at the three, hand-picked, Colorado Bar Association members who were sitting around his large, oak desk. Seated to his right was the most senior bar member of the appellate court system in Colorado, and the bar's legal adviser Dianne Tolmage. She simply stared back at Rick, while holding a piece of paper in her left hand which she set down on the desktop. He soon shifted his eyes to the second most senior member of the bar, Earl Black.

Earl was relatively young at fifty-six. He had blond hair, blue eyes and a trim body. He always dressed in something black everyday which had earned him the nickname around the bar as "The Second Man in Black." He always kept his hair pulled back into a ponytail and tucked inside of the suit jackets he wore in court.

The third person was the youngest member of the bar at twenty-eight. Her name was Kelly Joe, and she was sometimes very feisty in court. With a short frame of five feet, red hair and hazel eyes, she possessed a commanding voice when in the courtroom. She, like everyone else, was in business dress casual for this meeting.

"I don't think that I have to explain the need for possibly the next state attorney general from the 9th judicial district to get that position; do I?" asked Rick.

"No, you don't," said Kelly Joe speaking for all the others.

"That's good to know, have you heard anything, Earl?" asked Rick looking for any information.

"Nothing, yet, but they still have sixty days left in which to appeal their convictions."

"Thank you, Earl, what about you Dianne; have you heard anything, yet?"

"Nothing yet, either, but I will keep my eyes and ears open."

"Good, now I want to hear any options that you all can come up with for these people."

"Option A, they represent themselves in the appeals process and lose," said Earl, quickly.

"That would be a best-case scenario; another option?"

"They hire a knucklehead type of an attorney and lose," said Kelly Joe.

"I like that one, which we will call Option B, a second best-case scenario; another option?"

"They find and hire a very competent and resourceful attorney who gets their convictions overturned and legalizes same-sex marriages in the State of Colorado," said Dianne.

"How many attorneys in this state are capable of doing just that?" asked Rick.

"According to my insider information; three," said Dianne looking over her list that she had brought with her to the meeting.

"Give me that list," said Rick as he took the list that Dianne was handing him. As he looked over the list, he saw Attorney Daniel Marcos' name in the number three position.

The name that was in first position was a very good attorney, indeed. She was a former Colorado State Supreme Court associate justice, a former district court judge from Mesa County, a former district attorney from the 8th judicial district and former public defender in Montezuma County. She had twenty-seven years of legal expertise and experience which would make her a very formidable foe in the courtroom. Her name was Leslie Qwinland, and she was currently a criminal defense attorney in Meeker.

The second name on the list was equally powerful. Gary Spanichek was a former district court judge from Yuma County, a former prosecutor from the 11th judicial district, a former criminal defense attorney in the 16th judicial district and currently a public defender in Lake County. He had a total of twenty-two years of legal expertise and experience. Another formidable foe in the courtroom, but Rick knew he was weak-minded and easily controlled. Rick immediately determined that he wasn't a threat at all.

The last name on the list was definitely a formidable foe in the courtroom or in the lunchroom for that matter. Attorney Daniel Marcos had a total of twenty-one years of legal expertise and experience. He was a former prosecutor from the 15th judicial district, a former public defender from the City and County of Denver and currently a criminal defense attorney in the 6th judicial district. Rick knew that Daniel was the type of attorney who had taken on high risk and high profile clients in the past. All in all, seventy years of legal expertise and experience, as Rick set down the list on his desktop.

"I will control Gary as the head of the Bar, and I don't think that Leslie would take the appeals either."

"What makes you think that Leslie wouldn't take on their cases?" asked Kelly Joe, confused now.

"Two reasons, Kelly Joe. First, she's almost ready for retirement and I don't think she would throw her legal career down the drain over something like this. Second, she has a gay son, and that would be grounds for her recusal."

"And Daniel Marcos?" asked Dianne, concerned.

"The only way to control Daniel Marcos is to disbar him," said Rick, flatly.

"You don't think he would seriously take on their cases, do you?" asked Kelly Joe, now really confused.

"Yes, I do, Kelly Joe. Our supporters in the 4th judicial district wouldn't like getting same-sex marriages legalized here. As far as anyone is concerned, this meeting never happened; get out of here and call with news of any kind, good or bad."

"Rick," said Dianne as she was leaving.

"Yes?"

"The list I gave those people came from the computer, not me."

"I know, and I understand. It's not your fault," he said as the door closed.

Dianne returned to the front office of the Colorado Bar Association main office in Denver. She immediately looked up the phone number for Attorney Leslie Qwinland. She dialed the number she had on file; the phone rang twice before being answered.

"Thank you for calling the Law Offices of Qwinland and Darbin; how can I help you?" asked the voice, politely.

"This is Dianne Tolmage, may I speak to Mrs. Qwinland; it is urgent."

"One moment, please," said the voice as they paged Leslie; Leslie answered as the client she had been seeing was leaving.

"Yes?" asked Leslie pushing the PAGE button on her desktop phone.

"There's a Dianne Tolmage on the phone to speak to you; she says it is urgent."

All sorts of red flags went up in Leslie's mind.

"*What the hell does she want?*" thought Leslie, now very suspicious and defensive.

"Go ahead and put her through," said Leslie.

The connection was made and the person whom Dianne had spoken to, the law office's paralegal, walked back to Leslie's office to stand quietly in the office doorway while Leslie put Dianne on speakerphone.

"Good morning, Mrs. Qwinland, how are you doing today?" asked Dianne.

"Better, I had a really rough client in my office just before you called," said Leslie, lying through her teeth as the previous client was an eighty year old farmer with a land rights issue; hardly what anyone would consider a rough client.

"Sorry to hear that, Leslie, you have my sincere condolences."

"Why, thank you, Dianne, what can I do for you?" asked Leslie, now in full defensive mode.

"Has anyone contacted you recently about appealing their convictions?"

"What type of convictions?"

"Perhaps convictions on Domestic Violence, assault, etc.?"

"Yes, I received a letter from a couple of people in the Denver area about six weeks ago. I turned them down due to the nature of the appeals case."

"Good, did you recommend that they go see one of the other attorneys that were on the list that I gave them?"

"Yes, I did suggest two other, very good and very competent attorneys, here in the state."

"May I ask, who?"

"Gary Spanichek and Marcie Ludewig."

"Marcie Ludewig, from Grand Junction?" asked Dianne, a little confused now.

"Yes, and my next client is here; thank you for calling," she said hanging up the phone quickly.

"Why did you just lie to her? They were in your office last Tuesday."

"She doesn't need to know that; besides, I do have a letter from them just in case I am asked to produce one. Right now, go get us all some coffee, okay?"

"Okay, are you buying?"

"Of course," said Leslie, reaching for her purse and handing her paralegal a $20.00 bill.

When the person had left, she opened the safe in her office, withdrew a dark green colored, twelve inch by fifteen inch envelope from it and mailed it off during her lunch break at the courthouse. When Leslie returned to her office later on that afternoon, she sent an email to the current Colorado State Attorney General Sam Toole, in code. The email simply said, "The Titanic has risen and is setting sail for the Promised Land."

The email was received in the attorney general's office, but was seen by a member of the attorney general's staff. This staff member was being paid well to provide Rick Sanchez with any bits of unusual information, and this email was definitely unusual. The staff member made a hardcopy of the email and called Rick before entering the attorney general's office to deliver all the emails that had been received from the previous night.

Sam Toole, the current Colorado State Attorney General, was sitting back in his large, leather office chair. He was looking over the letters, emails, evidence packages and inmate appeals that came into his office daily. He was a sixty year old, silver-haired, heavyset, five feet six inch tall, man. He took off his dark blue, pinstriped, suit jacket and hung it up on the coat rack. His facial features hid well his Pacific Islander heritage. He had just opened up his office door when the person walked up to him.

"Yes, what is it?" asked Sam, looking down at his desktop.

"Just the regular afternoon mail and an unusual personal email from Attorney Leslie Qwinland."

"What makes this email so unusual? I get personal emails from most of the attorneys of this state."

"This message makes me think that she has lost her mind, sir."

"Very well, give me the message."

The paralegal handed Sam the email. Sam read the "No Subject" wording in the subject line of the email. He then looked to the bottom, left corner of the printout; there he saw the small, black star. The email had been copied before being presented to him.

"Take down this response."

The paralegal took out a pen from his left shirt pocket and a small pad of paper from his back, right pants pocket.

"Ready, Mr. Toole," the paralegal said with pen poised to write.

"We are experiencing radio problems. Is the captain aboard and are the fires in the boilers lit?" replied Sam as the person left.

Daniel had an early day for court as his last two afternoon cases had been continued for various reasons. He went back to the office to start reviewing the first appeals case. After he had finished reviewing the case, he reviewed the others which were very similar in nature. Shilah returned late to the office from his Durango court appearances.

"Shilah, can you do me a favor, please?" asked Daniel.

"Sure, what's that?" asked Shilah, grabbing a pen and small pad of paper from the top of his desktop.

"Find me the legal definitions of a civil union, an intimate relationship and a significant other."

"Okay, I'll have those definitions by Monday."

On the way home, Daniel called Cecilia and let her know that he had finished reviewing the case files and transcripts. He then went home and into the kitchen to fix everyone dinner. During the dinner preparation, he had to make a decision. This decision to take on the appeals cases wasn't going to be an easy one. During the night, Daniel realized what was truly at stake.

CHAPTER 3

Attorney Gary Spanichek returned to his office Monday morning and started going through all of his voicemail messages. He was immediately suspicious of the one from Rick Sanchez. After taking down the names and phone numbers of some potential clients, he called Rick. Gary then started going through his emails and found he had been copied on an email coming from Sam Toole going to Leslie Qwinland. He opened it up, printed out a copy to read later and deleted it while he waited on hold for Rick to get out of his meeting. Rick soon answered the phone, and during the meeting, he had been going through his emails as well.

"Hello, Gary, glad you called. By any chance, did you have some people in your office or did they contact you about appealing their convictions on Domestic Violence charges?"

"Yes, they were in my office a few weeks ago as I recall. I told them no after I reviewed their cases."

"That's the answer I wanted to hear; did you recommend anyone to them?"

"Yes, as I recall, I recommended Marcie Ludewig in Grand Junction and Della Mortam in Dillon."

"Thank you, Gary, and so sorry to have bothered you, goodbye," said Rick, hanging up the phone and feeling really confused by Marcie's name being used more than once and now Della Mortam's name had come up.

"Anytime, Rick; goodbye," said Gary, almost slamming down the phone and finally reading the emails.

Rick turned around and called Della Mortam.

"Good morning, Della, it's Rick with the Colorado Bar."

"What do you want, Mr. Sanchez?!" she barked at him over the phone while reading her emails. She was reading the one from Sam to Leslie and she didn't like the fact that Rick was calling.

"A little feisty this morning; is everything okay?"

"One of my clients was rearrested over the weekend," she said, knowing that it was a lie.

"I understand your frustration, it has happened to me a few times. Listen, the reason why I called you is, did you have some people either in your office or maybe they contacted you via email or regular mail about appealing their convictions on Domestic Violence charges?"

"Yes and I sent them away after I reviewed their cases."

"Good answer, Della. Do you happen to remember who you recommended them to go see?"

"Dave Morgan in Fountain, Molly Norman in Last Chance and Marcie Ludewig in Grand Junction."

"Thank you and goodbye," said Rick hanging up the phone and calling Dave next. Della yelled some obscenities at her phone after she had hung it up.

"Good morning Dave, its Rick," he said as someone in his office brought in a copy of the strange email he had been sent.

"Yes, Rick, what can I do for you?"

"Did you have some people contact you, either in person or via email or regular mail, about appealing their Domestic Violence convictions?"

"Yes and I after I reviewed their cases, I sent them away. Mark my words, if they find the right attorney in this state, and they will, you and your religious friends who are padding your pockets are going down along with that unconstitutional law."

"Thanks for the heads up, Dave. Did you recommend anyone to them?"

"Juliano Blatz would be a good place to start; goodbye," said Dave, hanging up the phone before Rick could say another word. Dave knew that it was a lie.

Rick took the email and looked it over. He couldn't make any sense out of the email so he tossed it into his paper shredder he kept under his desk. He then called Dianne in the outer office.

"Yes, Rick?"

"Could you bring me the files on Juliano Blatz, Molly Norman and Marcie Ludewig?"

"Right away."

A few minutes later, Dianne entered Rick's office with the requested files. He scanned over Molly's first and saw nothing in there that would indicate a threat to him or his friends. He closed her file and handed it back to Dianne. He looked over Juliano's record next and found some things in there that didn't sit well with him or would sit well with his friends.

Attorney Juliano Blatz was a former Federal Circuit Court judge from the 10th Federal Circuit Court in Denver. He was now a civil rights attorney at a small law firm in Longmont. He had taught law school classes in several colleges and one major university before becoming a Federal Circuit Court judge. He was currently teaching law school classes at Denver University in Denver. Rick handed the file back to Dianne who left the room; Rick then called Juliano.

"Good morning, Your Honor, by any chance did you have some people in your office or maybe they contacted you via email or regular mail about appealing their convictions on Domestic Violence charges?"

"Yes, about four months ago and I stepped down from the Bench years ago. I told them that if they couldn't find an attorney to file their appeals, that I would be only too happy to guide them in their quest."

"You wouldn't actually do the appeals for them? That's a little odd, Your Honor. Did you recommend any other attorneys?"

"Yes."

"Like who?"

"Marcie Ludewig, Molly Norman and Daniel Marcos among others."

Rick shifted uneasily in his seat at the mention of Daniel's name.

"Do you still teach those law school classes at DU?"

"Yes, on Tuesdays, Thursdays and Fridays in the evenings."

"What do you teach, Your Honor?"

"I teach Colorado and Federal Procedural Law on Tuesdays. On Thursdays I teach Civil Rights law and on Fridays, I teach Constitutional Law; goodbye," he said hanging up the phone.

27

Rick hung up his phone and knew that Juliano would be a formidable foe in the courtroom along with Daniel; he decided to call Daniel next.

Daniel had just poured himself a cup of coffee when Rick called. It was Shilah who answered the phone.

"Daniel, it's Rick from the Bar."

"Oh, that's just great; I wonder what I did this time. After the call, we will discuss your findings."

"I'm due at the Silverton Courthouse this morning, so I will just have to hand you my findings," he said, handing Daniel the paperwork. Daniel took the paperwork and set it all down on his desktop as he reached for the phone.

"Good morning, Rick, what can I do for you? Please make it quick, as I am very busy with clients this morning," said Daniel as he looked out across an empty office at the moment.

"Sure, I understand, so I will make this as quick as possible. Did you have some people contact you via email or regular mail? Maybe they came to see you in person to ask you to help them file an appeal for their convictions on Domestic Violence charges?"

"Yes, I'm reviewing their cases right now."

"Hurry it up and then drop them."

"Why?"

"Let their convictions stand; besides, they're worthless to society."

"Why do my potential clients make you so nervous on a simple appeal?" asked Daniel, now really suspicious of Rick's motives. He then hit the RECORD button on the side of the phone to record the rest of the conversation.

"You're playing with fire with those clients, and you're going to get very, very badly burned."

"Thanks for the heads up, Rick."

"Do not advocate for legalizing same-sex marriages in this state, do you hear me?"

"I hear you and I wouldn't dream of it. Besides, you and your friends have been able to get some bills through the legislature that took away the Colorado State Supreme Court's power to do things like that. You should be very proud of that accomplishment; now, why don't you tell me the real reason why my potential clients make you so nervous?"

"Your clients, you and three other attorneys in this state, make my friends very nervous. When they get nervous, I get nervous."

"You mean, your religious friends are getting nervous is more like it. Don't worry, as long as their Levitican laws stand unopposed, which they have for more than a decade now, you're safe."

"Let me make this very clear to you, if you advocate for legalizing same-sex marriages, you will be disbarred; don't even so much as mention the words in a sentence."

"And if a court of law asks me this type of a question?"

"No court of law in this state ever will; they know better than to discuss that issue in open court. No judges on the bench will either, except, of course, you and a few other attorneys that don't value their legal careers."

"Thanks for calling, and I'm going to think real hard about what you said, goodbye," said Daniel, hanging up the phone.

Rick had noticed that Dianne had been listening in on the whole conversation he had just completed. He walked over to shut his office door and saw her trying to make it look like she was working.

"Dianne, I know you were listening to what I said, don't be a fool."

"I don't know what you're talking about, Rick," she said, closing the four drawer filing cabinet that was to the right and behind her desk.

"I know that you're thinking you can help whomever it is to get same-sex marriages legalized, but don't, you'll just go down with them."

"I still don't know what you're talking about, Rick," she said trying to play it all off, but it wasn't working.

"I know that you have a same-sex marriage; we have friends in Kansas who provided me a copy of your same-sex marriage license; have a nice day," he said, closing the door to complete his other duties. Dianne was just leaving for lunch, when she turned around to see the Blind Lady of Justice holding the balanced scales on the wall of the main office.

"We could use a little help here, Madam," she said as she walked out the door to lunch.

Daniel stood up after reviewing the final case and started looking over all of his accomplishments of his legal career. There were pictures of Daniel with some of his clients after their high profile or high risk cases were over. There were pictures of Daniel with such people as current and former Colorado state legislators who were long since gone, at least two former governors and many judges.

Some of those judges were long since gone as well, but a few had decided that after retiring from the bench, Colorado would be a great place to start up a law firm. There were signed and framed letters of recognition and appreciation of Daniel's unrelenting work to help out those in the criminal justice process who were less fortunate. There were even letters of commendation from many law enforcement agencies and supporters.

Daniel turned from the front wall of his inner office which faced west to the east wall which was to his left. The east wall had all of his legal degrees, certifications and the few family photos he had collected over the years. There were pictures of him with Seth, Bill and Mr. and Mrs. Thompson. Then there were pictures with him and the boys. He saw all the happy vacation pictures and the wedding pictures from David's wedding; Seth's wedding pictures were, of course, absent.

He then saw his law school graduation pictures with him and his professor. As Daniel recalled, his law school professor thought Daniel wouldn't amount to much of anything. Daniel was snapped back to reality from his daydream with the opening of the outer office doors; Shilah was back from court already.

"Shilah, could you come into my office?" asked Daniel.

"Sure, Daniel, what's going on?"

Daniel sat down at his desk, picked up a pen that had been on his desktop and started twirling it around in his hands. He looked up at Shilah with tears getting ready to start flowing at any minute.

"Shilah, I need you to draw up paperwork to turn over all my legal cases to you. I'm not stupid; when I file this appeal, I will be disbarred."

"Are you trying to tell me that without just cause or a lot of censorship letters in your Bar file that the Bar is simply going to strip you of your certifications?"

"Yes, Rick called me a few minutes ago to threaten, intimidate and harass me into not taking on those people's appeals. Hopefully, I have taught you in the short time you have been with me that part of being a good criminal defense attorney is being able to see into the proposed future."

"It's not right and you know it. I know that I've only been here a short period of time, but in that short time you've taught me one thing."

"What's that?"

"Don't give up without a fight."

"I know, but at the present time, that is what is going to happen."

"I see, what effective date do you want me to put on the transfer of power?"

"The day this appeals case goes to the Colorado State Supreme Court."

"You really think it will go that far?"

"It may even end up on the doorsteps of the U.S. Supreme Court just like *Romer V. Evans*, 517 U.S. 620 did in 1996. This appeals case isn't just about my client's appealing their convictions; it's about my clients and the rest of the silent, fearful, LGBTQ community that calls Colorado home versus the religious stronghold of the United States."

"Which is Colorado?"

"Yes, and I am doing this alone all the way to the end if I am ordered to do so by my clients. When you get the paperwork drawn up, set it on my desktop, and I'll review it later."

"Sure, but Daniel, at least reconsider fighting hard for this one. If you're going to go down, don't let it be because you gave up. I promise to back you up in any way I can," he said as he left Daniel's office.

Daniel went down into the basement, opened the heavy vault door to his records vault and went inside. There, inside the records vault, in many, eight drawer filing cabinets, was his entire legal career both good and not so good. He then looked down on the floor and grabbed five empty boxes and took them back upstairs to his office.

He opened up his bottom, right desk drawer and grabbed the roll of shipping tape. After taping up all the boxes, he started taking down all of his awards, certificates and plaques. He placed them carefully into the boxes. When he had sealed up the last box, he took them all out to his car.

When the last box was in the car, he drove up the street to the museum he had helped found and went down into the old mine shaft to his special vault he had there. Bill had seen to it that before he died, Daniel would have a special place to keep all of his really special treasures of life. He put the boxes down there and returned to the office. Daniel checked his messages and found that Dave Morgan had called for him. Daniel sat down in his large, office chair and called Dave back.

"Daniel, did Rick Sanchez call you about some people wanting to appeal their criminal convictions?"

"Yes, Rick told me that I was playing with fire and that I was going to get very, very badly burnt if I continued with their appeals process."

"That bastard! Thank you, Daniel, for letting me know this and what is your middle name?"

"Santana; Dave, I know that I am going this route all alone because the few people in this state that do ally themselves with the LGBTQ community are no match for the Rick Sanchez religious war machine."

"Oh, I wouldn't say that, Daniel. You have lots of friends, Daniel and The Group will try and run as much interference as we possibly can. Can you give The Group some time?"

"How much time does this alleged Group need?"

"Don't file their appeal until the last day before the time clock runs out; goodbye, Daniel. I now have to rally the rest of The Group," said Dave as he hung up.

"Goodbye," said Daniel, hanging up the phone. As he was reviewing his emails, he was still thinking about what Dave had said to him.

"*The Group? What or who was The Group?*" Daniel thought.

Daniel completed reviewing his emails and called Brian Good-Smith about his emailed question.

"Hello Brian, it's Daniel, and I received your email. You asked a very good question."

"Thanks for calling, Daniel. I thought you might not take our appeals case."

"I'm glad you asked that, Brian. I just finished reviewing the cases this morning."

"Well, are we going to have to find another attorney? Or are you going to go through with the appeals process?"

"I'm trying to come up with a legal argument or arguments that I can use and I have some ideas. Your question can be answered like this. The government has access to an unlimited taxpayer funded war chest to use against you. In other words, the government will force you to quit at some point in time with the avalanche of paperwork they will have you and your attorney filing."

"I see, so are you telling me not to sue, then?"

"No, you have every right as a citizen of the State of Colorado and as a citizen of the United States to sue any governmental agency or governmental person, or both, if you so choose. It is called a Title 42, United States Code as Amended, Section 1983 case."

"Who would I sue, then, if I wanted to pursue this course of action?"

"The most likely state governmental agency to sue is the Colorado Department of Public Health and the Environment. The particular person to sue would be the Director of or for the Bureau of Vital Statistics."

"Why?"

"One reason for your lawsuit could be that the Colorado Defense of Marriage Act violates your rights, privileges and immunities granted to you as a citizen of the United States under the 14th Amendment, Section 1. The state, you could very easily show, also violated your rights under Article IV of the U.S. Constitution, Section 1 by not recognizing another state's public records."

"Why not that due process thing I keep hearing about all the time on TV?"

"The sections of both the 5th and 14th Amendment to the U.S. Constitution would be easily shown in a federal district court to be satisfied by the voter initiative process. It just so happens, not enough registered voters turned out in 2006 to defeat the initiative.

All I am asking you to do is, hold off on the lawsuit until after this appeals case goes the full round."

"Thanks for calling, Daniel; goodbye," said Brian, hanging up the phone and feeling both hurt and angry at the same time.

After dinner, Daniel called Todd and Chayton together for a family meeting. Todd was getting upset because he thought for sure that Daniel had found the dozen or so boxes of condoms in his room. When everyone was seated at the table, Todd spoke first.

"Dad, I have a confession to make. All those boxes of condoms you found in my room that day, are all mine."

"I figured they were yours, but that's not the reason why we are all here at the table."

"Dad, I also learned in school that it used to be illegal to sell condoms to people my age."

Before Daniel could answer, Chayton spoke.

"Dad, is he lying?" asked Chayton with a serious look on his face.

"No Chayton, he isn't lying. In the State of New York in the mid 1970's, it was illegal to sell contraceptives to anyone under the age of 16. The case was called *Carey V. Population Services, International* 431 U.S. 678. The U.S. Supreme Court struck down the law as being unconstitutional under both the 1st and 14th Amendments, as I recall."

"Well, why are we here then?" asked Todd, feeling much more relieved now.

"I am going to file the appeal in the cases of those people that came into my office a few weeks ago. Sooner or later, it's going to get out into the press that I filed their appeals case. We will become targets of hate crimes, harassment, intimidation, bullying, death threats and assaults to name a few things. If there is anything that has any value for you at this house, box it up and I'll take it to the mountain storage area where it will be safe."

"Dad, why does someone want to hurt us?" asked Chayton.

"When the religious stronghold of the United States finds out who is representing the appealers in their appeals case, the hate will flow heavily. I've already been threatened with disbarment if I keep up the appeals process."

"Why, Dad?" asked Todd.

"I am one of four attorneys that the religious stronghold fears because I might find the weaknesses in the nearly perfect patchwork of laws that they have passed and exploit them in open court."

"So, drop their case, Dad," said Todd.

"I'm not going to drop their case, Todd, because I know that I can win. You take for granted your intimate relationships with your many girlfriends, right?"

"Of course; so?"

"My clients were stripped of that right and privilege, or whatever you wish to call it, when they came to this state. If you were in their shoes, I would like to think that if someone stripped you of the right you now take for granted, you would be upset."

"Of course I would be upset; who wouldn't. But, Dad, what if you lose?"

"Then I lose it all and go home a broken and disgraced attorney because I stood up for not only my client's rights, but for the rights of hundreds of thousands like them that live in this state under constant silence and fear."

"What would you do then, Dad?" asked Todd.

"Work up at the museum as a tour guide. I have made some wonderfully wise investments following some great advice from Bill at the bank before he died, and I have many more millions of dollars."

"Dad, what crime did these people do?" asked Chayton.

"The word is called commit. The only crimes that my client's committed were falling in love with someone of the same sex and then marrying them prior to coming to this state."

"Get rid of those clients, Dad. They can find some other attorney to handle their appeals case," said Todd, boldly.

"They don't have anybody else but me to defend them. Chayton, did you once tell me that there are those in this world that need a hero?" asked Daniel as he fixed his eyes squarely on Todd.

"Yeah."

"Here's my chance; do I become a hero, and possibly throw it all away? Or do I run and hide with my tail tucked between my legs like a COWARD?" asked Daniel, with the emphasis on the last word.

"They need a hero, Dad; go for it," said Chayton, smiling ear to ear.

"And what about you, Todd?"

"I'm against it for personal safety issues among other reasons."

"Your dissenting opinion has been duly noted; everyone off to bed."

CHAPTER 4

The chief justice of the Colorado State Supreme Court was completing his fourth round of the six rounds of chemotherapy and radiation treatments for his particular form of cancer. He had just put on his clothes at the hospital when his doctor came in to the dressing area to talk to him. When the doctor entered, the judge threw up into a bed pan.

"I've got good news for you, Your Honor. The latest test results seem to indicate the cancer is going into remission," he said, knowing that it wasn't true.

"That's great, as my hair is falling out and I've lost more than forty pounds."

"Your hair will return after the radiation treatments end in May of 2021."

"And my skin looks like leather and sometimes I don't eat for weeks after these treatments."

"I can give you a prescription for a different type of anti-nausea drug."

"Nothing has worked, so give it up."

The doctor knew that the judge was referring to a drug list he had submitted earlier during the treatments.

"I can't give you some of the drugs on that list you gave me because they are illegal in the United States for various reasons. You're allergic to Marinol®; let me see if some of the pharmaceutical companies here in the U.S. can get one of those other anti-nausea drugs from their European or Asian counterparts."

"Yeah, all right, see you in March," he said, leaving, knowing he didn't have much time left. He returned to his office to continue writing opinions and to complete the nomination list for the governor with whom he had an appointment with later that day.

It was late Friday afternoon when Earl received a copy of the nominations list from his contact at the governor's office. The Chief Justice's list was short with only five names on it. He saw the last name on the list, Daniel S. Marcos; he deleted the copy from his personal e-mail after he printed it out. Earl took his copy over to Rick's office. Rick looked over the list, completely ignoring the other names and focused on Daniel's. He set the list down and smiled as he turned around to his computer. He typed on the keyboard for a few minutes, printed out what he typed and handed the press release to Earl.

"We're always ready with contingency plans. Make sure that press release gets into Monday morning's edition in print, TV and Internet."

"Right away," said Earl as he left the office as Rick was putting the e-mail printout through the shredder.

David sent out two e-mails to Leslie, who was providing the guidance for The Group. She was getting ready to leave her office for the weekend when the e-mails arrived. She saw them both, but then decided to print them out to read them over the weekend. When she arrived at home, she read the e-mails. The first one was great news, but the second one was definitely bad news. Leslie destroyed both e-mails and deleted them before driving from Meeker to Frisco to call Sam. Sam came to his other cell phone when his son told him who was calling.

"Leslie, the ship has to get underway right now, if the enemy has already fired the first shot; she is a sitting duck at anchorage."

"I understand your concern, Sam, but she won't have full steam pressure in the boilers for fifteen more days."

"The ship has to get underway immediately, and tell the captain to take evasive action, once he is in open water."

"I'll start decoy operations and I'll make sure that the enemy runs into lots of icebergs."

"Keep me posted; goodbye," said Sam, hanging up the phone as Leslie drove back to Meeker to await further news.

Daniel was packing up some clothes for him and Chayton. He was driving to Hot Sulfur Springs to meet his clients. The kids all went to play in the pool, while Daniel talked to his clients in the hotel's state room.

"I'm glad you could all come up here and I'm glad you brought along your kids because this concerns them as well," said Daniel.

"Are things getting rough for you, Daniel?" Patricia asked.

"Yes and I want you to know that at any time, you can tell me to stop this appeals process, and I will; no questions asked."

"Oh hell no, we're going all the way; Daniel," said Adam, quickly.

"Let me put this into perspective for you and your kids. If we go all the way, this case is more than likely going to the United States Supreme Court."

"Are you serious?" asked John with large eyes and no smile on his face.

"Yes, I took an oath over two decades ago as an attorney that despite my personal feelings, I would defend those who are defenseless or, in your cases, oppressed."

"What are your personal feelings on our cases?" asked Cecilia.

"Cecilia, there is a high probability that my son, Seth, may be in a same-sex marriage. If he is, then in the eyes of some in my profession, that is grounds for disbarment, because it could be shown that I was taking your appeals cases personally."

Daniel paused before continuing, as Cecilia was typing something on her cell phone.

"When the press finds out who has filed your appeals case, you, your kids, your property, your coworkers, neighbors, friends, relatives, etc., will become targets for hate crimes, assaults, death threats, etc. If you haven't taken hand-to-hand combat courses yet, now is a good time to start."

Daniel paused before speaking again.

"If you don't own any firearms, get some and train with them. If you don't have your conceal carry permits, get them now."

"Do you think it is going to get that bad, Daniel?" asked Brian, very concerned now.

"Yes, because you live in a state that is considered by many people in the world to be the religious stronghold of the United States of America."

"I told you he would figure it out, John," said Tom, looking at him.

"Yes, I figured it out on the way down here. Now, your kids might need to start taking hand-to-hand combat courses as they will become the targets. Do you still want me to continue with the appeals process?"

They all nodded their heads.

"Please be aware that your kids will be interviewed by the press. They need to be careful about what they say."

"We will talk to our kids. They pretty much know what to say and what not to say," said Cecilia.

"I hope so, if they say the wrong thing to the press, it will more than likely ruin your appeals case. Now, I want to talk to the older kids."

Everyone left the room and the kids over fourteen filed into the room and sat down, still wet from the pool.

"Let me tell you that I know your mothers and fathers love you very much. But, you need to protect the younger ones from the press as best you can. The other kids are going to try and pick fights with all of you, say bad things about your parents, and when they do, expect cameras to be taking pictures and/or shooting video; there will be microphones everywhere."

"Are you trying to scare us?" asked one of them.

"No, you're about to become possible victims of hate crimes, assaults, harassment, verbal abuse, property damage, etc. I have a feeling that when I file this appeals case for your parents, the judge is going to want you in the courtroom. All courtrooms, because of the Proposition 8 trial case from the 9th Federal Circuit Court years ago, are equipped with cameras. Anyone logging onto the website for the Colorado courts is going to be able to see you."

"That means anyone logging in will know what we look like," said another one, dejectedly.

"That's right, and now would be a good time for you to get all of your friends together for the forthcoming battles."

"What makes you think we have any friends here?" asked another one.

"If my calculation is correct, you should have more than 605,000 friends in this state. Use them to impede the progress of those who wish to hurt you or your younger siblings."

"Like a human shield?" asked yet another.

"Yes, and if a news reporter is asking you questions, I suggest not talking to them; they can't print the truth. Simply walk away and tell them 'no comment', 'leave me alone', 'I don't want to talk to you', etc."

The kids all talked amongst themselves and then Daniel let them go. He then showered and changed into his swimming trunks to go swimming with everyone else. On the way back home on Sunday night, the Monday morning editions of many prominent newspapers in the state of Colorado were being put together. The *Ironton Gazette* printed up a front page headline with the nomination of Daniel as possibly the next chief justice of the Colorado State Supreme Court. The next morning, as Daniel arrived at work, there were about a dozen reporters, including news crews from channels 7 and 25 in Denver. Daniel looked right at Mary from the *Ironton Gazette*, very sternly.

"So, Mary, do I owe you the honor of a thank you for this wonderful Monday morning reception at my office?" asked Daniel, smiling for the video cameras and flashing digital cameras.

"Yes, when I saw the headline from Denver, I called a few friends," she replied, while holding the morning edition of the newspaper. She handed it to Daniel who took it into his left hand. Before he could open it up, a video camera was thrust into his face along with a microphone and a reporter.

"Mark Walston, Channel 7 news, Denver. How does it feel to be on the outgoing chief justice's nomination list?" he asked.

"What are you talking about?" asked Daniel, a little uneasy now.

"Is it true that if you are nominated to the bench, you would legalize same-sex marriages?" he asked.

"Absolutely not; those things will never be legal in the state without divine intervention."

"Sally Wise, Channel 25 news, Denver. How come you didn't say the words same-sex marriage?" she asked.

"I'm under orders, from my superiors, not to say those words."

"Who are you talking about?" she asked.

"Rick Sanchez of the Colorado Bar comes to mind, right now."

"Were you aware that you were on the judge's nomination list?" asked Mark.

"No, I wasn't aware that I was on his list; I am glad he thought of me, though."

Daniel started ignoring the others and finally opened up the paper. The headline was certainly eye-catching. 'HIGH-PROFILE ATTORNEY ON CHIEF JUSTICE'S NOMINATION LIST.' He read the article briefly before putting the paper down on the desktop where Lynn used to sit. The reporters from channels 7 and 25 followed Daniel into his inner office. They were setting up for an exclusive interview.

"This is my inner office, and my office rules are simple; if you ask a question I don't like, you leave," said Daniel.

"Okay," said Mark with his microphone in hand; Daniel casually sat on the right corner of his desk.

"Mr. Marcos, what are your views on the 2nd amendment?" asked Mark.

"It is an individual right in accordance with the U.S. Supreme Court's rulings."

"Could you legalize same-sex marriages, if you were appointed as the next possible chief justice of the Colorado State Supreme Court?" asked Sally.

"First of all, that position is an elected one, and I have no intentions of running for office. Second of all, since I have no political ambitions, I would make a terrible Chief Justice."

Everyone started laughing at this comment.

"I asked you a question, Justice Marcos; would you legalize same-sex marriages if you were appointed to the bench?" asked Sally, rather loudly.

"The Colorado State Supreme Court can't do anything like that anymore, thanks to the legislature. There were good reasons why the governor's, during their respective administrations, vetoed those bills. But the good old boys in the legislature saw to it that there were enough votes to override the vetoes."

"Just one more question, Justice Marcos, do you think that the Defense of Marriage Act, which is now part of the Colorado State Constitution, is, perhaps, unconstitutional?" asked Sally.

Daniel looked over at her and then at the other reporters.

"That question went over the line; the interview is over, and everyone can leave my inner office," said Daniel, smiling and showing all the reporters out the door.

He returned to his office and found the red message light on his phone was flashing three consecutive times in a row. To Daniel that meant his office was 'bugged' now. He looked around, closed the shades and started to visually search the office for the 'bug.'

Silently he opened the wall safe, and withdrew an electronic device from the safe. He then quietly turned around in the room. There, on the underside of his desk, was the 'bug'; he immediately destroyed the thing. He returned the device to the safe, but the message light was still flashing. Now Daniel knew his phone had been tapped. The phone started ringing as Daniel picked it up.

"Hello?" asked Daniel.

"Hello, is Daniel there?"

"Yes, who is this?"

"Dave, from Fountain."

"Dave Morgan?"

"Yes."

"Good to hear from you, Dave. It's been about six years now since we last spoke to each other, right?"

"Yes."

"Dave, be very careful what you say to me."

"I understand; we all know that you're a very smart man."

"I certainly hope so."

"You're to get underway immediately. Once the ship is underway into open water, take evasive actions."

"I understand; goodbye."

Rick was in his office looking over the transcripts of Dave's phone call to Daniel. He was looking at the man who had tapped Daniel's phone lines. Rick wasn't at all amused by this waste of time and money.

"Do you have any idea what that means?" asked Rick to the man.

"Not a clue, Rick. Perhaps they're playing a computer video game that requires this type of a conversation."

"You could say that, but most computer video games over the Internet have a chat capability; keep listening, and I need a favor."

"What's that?"

"I want you to get me a copy of Seth Thompson-Marcos' same-sex marriage license. A little birdie told me that Toronto, Canada, would be a great place to look."

"Yes, sir, did you want a certified copy?"

"By all means and bill me for it; goodbye, sir," said Rick, showing the man out the door.

Daniel was going through his e-mails, when he came across one from Leslie. It read, "Welcome aboard, skipper! As your executive officer, I will be with you until the end of this journey at New York Harbor. You can call me XO for short; looking forward to getting underway. But, first I must check on our passengers, crew and the enemy; goodbye."

Daniel deleted the message and prepared his arguments for the appeals process. After printing up the hardcopy, he mailed it off to the clerk of the court for appeals within the 2nd judicial district. Dave rescheduled his court appointments and drove up to Denver to see Sam, as it was an emergency. Sam, although he was due in court shortly, saw Dave right away. Dave waited until the office door was shut before he turned on some music and closed the blinds.

"What's going on, Dave?" asked Sam.

"Someone is monitoring Daniel's office line. He told me, thankfully, before I told him what to do; I had to tell him in code."

"Do you think he will file that appeals case today?"

"Daniel's a smart man; he'll figure it out."

"If I find out that Rick had anything to do with any illegal wiretaps on Daniel without probable cause, I'll see to it that he goes to prison for a very long time."

"Rick could call it okay under the Electronic Monitoring provisions of the USA PATRIOT ACT III."

"He might, but he probably isn't aware that the U.S. Supreme Court struck down that part of the USA PATRIOT ACT III as being unconstitutional in that the way it is worded makes it invasive. I believe Associate Justice Fallon called it too invasive in the wording of the 4th Amendment."

"What's the next step?"

"We can only wait to see if Daniel filed the appeals case today or not. Tell Juliano that the time has come for plan A1 from him."

"Will do; goodbye," said Dave, rushing out of Sam's office. Dave drove home and called Juliano, from one of the public libraries of Douglas County in the town of Castle Rock, on his cell phone.

"Yes, Dave, what can I do for you?" asked Juliano as he was preparing Tuesdays lecture and grading student papers.

"I just came from an emergency meeting with Sam. He told me to tell you to go ahead with plan A1."

"Okay, plan A1 it is, then; goodbye," he said, hanging up the phone.

Juliano finished writing the lecture and completed grading the student's term papers. The next morning, when he arrived at his law office, he opened his office safe, and removed a large, red envelope which was pre-addressed to the local office of the United States District Attorney General. On his way to court that day, he stopped by the post office and mailed the envelope. Juliano then sent a quick text message to Sam that read, "Countermeasures have been dispatched per instructions. Need lots of icebergs to slow up the enemy until reinforcements arrive later." He then turned his cell phone off before going into court.

Daniel had spent most of the night looking up the myriad of definitions of what was considered evasive actions. He also reviewed many hours of video evidence of what different types of evasive actions he could take. Throughout all of the video evidence he watched, one theme seemed clear. Dodge incoming enemy fire!

CHAPTER 5

The clerk of the court for appeals within the 2nd judicial district for the City and County of Denver, Colorado, received the Certified Mail® envelope which contained the appeals case from Daniel on behalf of his clients. He then started opening up all of the appeals cases, one by one. He went through them all to make sure that they were complete, which included making sure that all the proper and correct forms were attached.

He then went back through all of them a second and third time to make sure that all of them were within the time frame allowed for appeals by Colorado Revised Statutes. After this was completed, he had to reject one hundred ten of the five hundred plus appeals cases for various reasons. He prepared the rejection letters and clearly stated on what grounds the rejection was based upon.

The clerk then took the stack of appeals cases down the hallway to the head appeals court judge, Judge Randall Bach. The clerk knocked on the double wooden doors that marked the entrance to the judge's chambers; when Judge Bach opened the door, the clerk handed the judge the stack of paperwork and the judge disappeared into his chambers.

Inside of Randall's chambers were the judges of the appeals court. Randall noted that Divisions U, V, W, Y and Z were represented. Judge Donna Pinewood, Division X was still in court awaiting the jury's verdict in a very complicated civil law suit. The other judges quickly assessed the appeals cases and assigned them to their respective colleagues. When the appeals case that

Daniel had filed came up for assignment, Randall immediately took personal charge of the case and assigned it to Judge Pinewood.

Judge Bach was a tall man at six feet six inches in height. He always wore business dress clothes and was frequently seen wearing a suit coat or jacket and a tie. He was of thin build at about one hundred fifty-five pounds, with brown hair and eyes. His hair had recently started to show his age with streaks of gray showing up intermittently in the brown. This was a testimony to the forty plus years on the bench. The clerk waited patiently for about an hour before Judge Bach opened his chamber door again.

"Clerk Osborne, on the case of *Cecilia Duffy-Downs Et. Al. V. The State of Colorado*, give that case to Judge Donna Pinewood in Division X."

"Yes, Your Honor," he replied, a little confused as Judge Pinewood only did civil cases and was very good at them.

The clerk went back to his office and started putting the electronic stamps on the appeals cases showing the date and time of receipt. Next, he started putting them through an electronic stamping machine which put the dates and times for their respective hearings on them. When this was done, he started distributing the cases to their respective judges. His final duty was mailing out the notification letters to the parties in the appeals cases. He had just finished that duty off when Judge Pinewood walked into his office.

Judge Donna Pinewood was one of the youngest judges on the appeals bench at just thirty-three years of age. She was five feet nine inches tall, with black hair and blue eyes. She weighed about one hundred twenty-five pounds and wore large, wire framed glasses. Her appeals specialty was civil cases, so she was very confused by the criminal case that was now on her docket. She had a copy of the docket in her hand when she started speaking to the clerk of the court.

"This has to be a mistake; I don't do criminal appeals cases."

"I know that, Your Honor. Judge Bach told me to give that one to you."

"I see, is he in his chambers?"

"Yes."

"Thank you," she said marching out of the clerk's office and down the hall. The clerk called ahead to warn Judge Bach of her arrival. Then he went down the opposite hall to the janitor's closet to call Sam Toole. The clerk used his personal cell phone to make the call.

"Yes, Mr. Osborne, what can I do for you?" asked Sam from his office on his personal cell phone instead of the state issued one he carried most of the time. Sam had locked his office door for security reasons.

"The Titanic is underway, heading for the Promised Land."

"Are you sure?"

"Yes, sir, the Dashing, Suave, Man About Town weighed anchor this morning at 10:30 a.m."

"When is the date?"

"November 1st, 2020 at 8:30 a.m. in Judge Pinewood's courtroom."

"Division X?"

"Yes, sir."

"Good work; goodbye," said Sam as he hung up the phone and the clerk returned to his office.

Judge Bach was staring at Judge Pinewood.

"Your Honor, my specialty is civil law, not criminal law. As you know, I didn't do very well in the oral boards in criminal law; why did I end up with a criminal law appeals case?" she asked, trying not to show how upset she was.

"With the case load this quarter being heavier than usual, I have over seventy-five cases myself. There was only one criminal case left and that's why I assigned it to you. As you know, it is my policy to make sure that the quarterly duty judge has the lightest possible docket. This is in case they have to sign search warrants, etc."

"I see."

"In case you're wondering, the attorney who filed that appeals case is known to you."

"He is?" said Donna looking through the case file quickly.

"Yes, Attorney Daniel Marcos, Esquire."

"Oh, I see now."

"And, make sure, no matter what he says in court, that you uphold the trial court's decision."

"Okay, I will think about it, Your Honor. And if he wants to appeal my decision?"

"Let him know that the appeal will be a three judge panel consisting of myself, Judge Haryln and Judge Bowls."

"I will let him know that if he decides to appeal his case further, and I understand that I must uphold the lower court's decision; goodbye, Your Honor," she said as she left Judge Bach's chambers, a little perplexed by his request to her on a case she would have to hear first; she then stopped by the clerk's office.

"Did you call ahead to warn Judge Bach that I was coming?" she asked.

"No, Your Honor, I did not."

"Somehow I don't believe you; you're not a very good liar," she said, returning to her chambers to review the cases she had. The last case she reviewed was case number 20AP7719. When she saw who the prosecutor had been on all three of those cases, she understood why Judge Bach wanted her to uphold the lower court's decision. The prosecutor was the man running for the office of the Colorado State Attorney General, Richard Kilam.

Rick was in his office when the man returned. He was just getting off the phone with Judge Bach. The man closed the door behind himself and dropped a plain, manila-colored envelope down on the desktop. Rick covered the phone's microphone before putting Randall on hold so that he could talk to the man without the judge hearing the conversation.

"Is it Daniel's son, Seth's, same-sex marriage license?" asked Rick excitedly, looking at the Canadian post office stamp in the middle, top portion of the envelope. Rick then looked at the return address label which was from the Toronto office of Vital Statistics.

"Yes, I am certain of it."

"How much?"

"$300 Canadian Dollars plus overnight delivery costs."

Rick opened up the envelope, removed the contents and looked it over. He was satisfied that it was the real thing. Next, he pulled out a black marker from his, suit jacket pocket and grabbed a sticky notepad. Rick scribbled the words, "NICE TRY CHIEF JUSTICE MARCOS!" and made the unhappy face underneath it. He put the note in with the marriage license and put it back into the envelope.

Rick then opened up the top, center drawer to his desk and handed the man a legal size envelope which contained $500.00 cash. The man took the envelope, counted the money, smiled and left the office; Rick then took the judge back off of hold.

"Thank you, Your Honor, for letting me know he appealed their convictions. I will make sure he meets some resistance; goodbye," he said, hanging up the phone. He then walked out to speak to Dianne.

"Dianne, can you get me Attorney Kenneth Fargo on the phone for me? I think he's with the Law Firm of Smith, Gold and Karnes."

"Yes, Rick," she said, picking up the phone.

Attorney Kenneth Fargo was the fifth youngest attorney at the Law Firm of Smith, Gold and Karnes, as he was only twenty-seven. He was of average height and thin build, weighing less than one hundred thirty pounds. He had sandy blond hair, which he kept closely trimmed at all times and blue eyes.

He was also an attorney who was not afraid to take on some of the more powerful and respected attorneys in the Denver area in the courtroom. He had also won eight out of his last ten cases and was able to get one dismissed on a legal technicality. He answered his phone as he was preparing to go to court that morning for several clients.

"Hello?" he asked as he set down his stack of papers.

"Is this Kenneth Fargo?" asked Dianne.

"Yes."

"Stand by for Rick Sanchez," she said as there was an audible click on the line.

"Mr. Fargo, I'm calling in that favor from a few months ago."

"Yes, Mr. Sanchez, what can I do for you?"

"I need you to represent the State of Colorado in an appeals case against a very well known, very thorough criminal defense attorney who doesn't give up easily."

"I understand; when?"

"November 1st, 2020 at 8:30 a.m., the appeals court for the 2nd judicial district for the City and County of Denver Division X. I believe that Division X is Her Honor Judge Donna Pinewood's courtroom. Before you go into the courtroom, I want you to stop by my office; I have something for you to give to the other attorney."

"Yes, Mr. Sanchez and who is this other attorney I am going up against in Judge Pinewood's courtroom?"

"Daniel Marcos, Esquire."

"Oh, he is a very, very good attorney from what I have heard from some of the senior members of the law firm. He seems to specialize in high risk or high profile clients."

"Yes, your information is correct about him; thank you and goodbye," said Rick, hanging up the phone.

Daniel was going through his mail when he picked up the brightly colored envelope. The envelope felt very heavy, so he set it aside on his desktop so he could review it later. He then went through the rest of his mail. Several of the letters to him, oddly enough, contained hate messages directed at him for taking on his client's appeals case. He filed the hate mail away in one of the office filing cabinets. Daniel then opened up the heavy envelope and removed the contents.

The contents were a spiral bound notebook, which was labeled as "THE TITATNIC CAPTAIN'S HANDBOOK" and a short letter from Dave Morgan about the book. Daniel set the letter down on his desktop and called Dave.

"Hello, Dave, its Daniel Marcos. I received your package today and I will read it whenever I'm not in court."

"That's good news; please read it carefully as it contains some helpful insights in dealing with the religious right group."

"Don't worry, I will; by the way, who else knows about this appeals case and its uniqueness outside of the courts?"

"No one that I know of; why?" asked Dave on alert now.

"I just started receiving fan mail here, and it isn't very nice."

"Hate mail already?"

"Yes."

"I understand, and you know what to do if any of that hate mail contains death threats?"

"Notify law enforcement immediately; goodbye," said Daniel, hanging up the phone as he started going through his email now. His email contained hate mail as well.

Daniel's last email was from the clerk of the court of the 2nd judicial district appeals Division X. The email contained the usual legal stuff and then he saw who the judge was going to be; Her

Honor Donna Pinewood. He also saw what he feared; his clients and their kids were required to be in the courtroom. He then saw the last part of the email, "This case will be broadcast on Colorado courts TV as required by the court directives of the 9th Federal Circuit Court as issued from the Proposition 8 Trial in 2010."

Daniel printed up the email before sending it to his clients. He then started preparing his opening statements and making travel arrangements. When the travel arrangements were completed, for the one day that he expected to be in Denver, he asked Shilah to watch Todd and Chayton.

As the weeks went by, the animosity towards Todd and Chayton mounted at the school they attended. Daniel still had not received any death threats, but his office had been vandalized several times. Sexually explicit graffiti was spray-painted on his vehicle a couple of times. His office was even torched twice a little less than a week before he went to Denver. To make matters worse, the outside of his house had been vandalized the day before he was to be in Denver.

Daniel was waiting to clear security when his personal cell phone rang; he saw that it was Chayton who was calling. When Daniel answered the phone, he could tell that Chayton was upset and crying. Some of his school friends were saying really mean and ugly things about him and his father; Daniel did his best to calm him down.

"Chayton, I want you to relax and listen to what I have to say. Those kid's parents are teaching them that hate is an acceptable family value."

"But hate is wrong, Dad," he said, sobbing.

"That's right, now get back into class, and I will try and be home tonight."

"Okay, Dad, goodbye."

Daniel shut off both of his cell phones and cleared security. He found Division X of the appellate court for the 2nd judicial district on the fifth floor of the new courthouse. He saw the familiar sign on the outside of the door "QUIET COURT IN SESSION," so he opened the back doors to the courtroom slowly to discover that the previous case wasn't over with, yet. The back doors closed and then opened up once again as Mr. Fargo entered the courtroom, taking a seat in the spectator's box on the opposite side from Daniel, waving at him. Daniel smiled and waved back. The Bailiff stood up when Donna banged down her gavel.

"All rise," said Sandy the Bailiff, as Judge Pinewood left the courtroom by the front doors which were to the left of her bench.

Sandy started readjusting the cameras so that they looked right where Daniel was setting up his stuff. She then readjusted the cameras that faced Mr. Fargo and, then readjusted the remaining cameras so that Daniel's client's kids could be clearly seen. Daniel visited a short time with his clients before Mr. Fargo interrupted them. Mr. Fargo had opened up his briefcase and removed the envelope that he had picked up from Rick earlier that morning. Mr. Fargo tossed the envelope down in front of Daniel. Daniel opened up the envelope and removed the contents. The contents were Seth's same-sex marriage license from Toronto, Canada and Rick's note; Daniel looked over at Mr. Fargo.

"Where did you get this?"

"From Rick Sanchez this morning, before coming to court; he told me to give it to you."

"Well, that was mighty nice of him. You tell Rick thank you for clearing up a suspicion that I have had for almost four years now."

"Will do," replied Kenneth, now a little confused by the statement.

Daniel saw the note, but ignored it for the time being, tossing it into his briefcase for later viewing. As the Bailiff stood up, so did everyone else.

"All rise, the 2nd judicial district for the City and County of Denver in the State of Colorado, Appellate Court, Division X, is now in session. The Honorable Judge Donna Pinewood, presiding, over the case of *Cecilia Duffy-Downs Et. Al. V. The State of Colorado.* Case number 20AP7719."

Donna seated herself at her bench, banging down her gavel twice for some unknown reason. Daniel detected this as a sign that something wasn't right for the judge. She then put on her reading glasses as she opened up the case file.

"You may be seated and this court will come to order," she said as the rest of the courtroom sat down.

She cleared her throat several times before continuing.

"This is the appeals hearing for case number 20AP7719. This appeals case is a combined appeals case of criminal case numbers 20CR1999, 20CR2000 and 20CR2001. In accordance with the 9th Federal Circuit Court ruling from the Proposition 8 trial, these proceedings are being broadcast on TV. Does either party have an objection to these proceedings being broadcast on TV?"

Daniel stood up immediately; he knew something was very wrong, now.

"No objections, Your Honor," he said, sitting back down.

Mr. Fargo stood up.

"No objections, Your Honor," he said, sitting back down.

"So noted; hearing no objections from either party, these proceedings will be made available to anyone requesting a copy of these proceedings, whether hardcopy or digital copy, in accordance with Title 5, United States Code as Amended, Section 552, the Freedom Of Information Act for a reasonable reproduction fee. Does either party have an objection to what I just said?"

Daniel stood up, now very much concerned that this appeals case wasn't going to get a fair hearing from Judge Pinewood.

"No objections, Your Honor," he said, sitting back down.

Mr. Fargo stood up.

"No objections, Your Honor," he said, sitting back down.

"So noted; hearing no objections from either party, these proceedings will be broadcast at www.ColordoCourtsTV.gov/2JD/DivisionX/DMP/20AP7719 as well as TV channels 454 and 429. Is the State of Colorado represented in these proceedings in this courtroom?" she asked, looking very nervous now from Daniel's point of view.

Mr. Fargo stood up.

"The State of Colorado is represented in your courtroom, Your Honor," he said while he remained standing.

"So noted; would you clearly state your name and who you work for, for the court records?"

"I am Kenneth Fargo, currently working with the Law Firm of Gold, Smith and Karnes. I have been retained by the State of Colorado to represent their interest in this appeals case," he said, sitting back down at his table.

"Thank you, Mr. Fargo. Is there legal representation for the appealers? Or do they still have their court appointed attorney present?"

Daniel stood up now, trying to figure out why Donna was going through such painstaking efforts to follow all of the courtroom procedures as if it was her first day in the courtroom by herself as a new judge; this set Daniel on full alert.

"The appealers are represented, Your Honor," said Daniel, standing up and remaining that way.

"So noted; would you clearly state your name and who you work for, for the court records?"

"Yes, Your Honor. I am Daniel Marcos of the Law Firm of Marcos and Haynes, LLC. I have been retained by the appealers to represent them in these proceedings," said Daniel, sitting back down. He then quickly wrote something down a small piece of paper he had sitting in front of him and handed it to Cecilia. She took the note and put it into her purse.

"So noted, is the State prepared with their side of the appeals case?"

"We are, Your Honor," said Ken, standing up.

"So noted; is opposing counsel for the appealers ready to proceed?"

"We are, Your Honor," said Daniel, standing up and remaining that way.

"So noted; before we go any further, there will be no other record of these proceedings in any form to include text messaging, video messaging, etc. If you do not have any business with the court on this particular case, you are instructed to leave the courtroom immediately. Bailiff, at this time you're hereby ordered to confiscate from everyone who remains in this court room, their cell phones, PDA's or other electronic mediums; you will get them all back at the end of this case."

The Bailiff had quite the collection when she had collected the last ones including Daniel's two cell phones, laptop, and digital recorder, which had been cleverly disguised as an ink pen.

"Thank you, Bailiff. At this time, this court will take a five minute recess before the State begins its opening statement," she said, banging down her gavel twice again before leaving the courtroom, visibly shaking.

"All rise," said Sandy.

It was ten minutes later that Judge Pinewood returned to her courtroom. Everyone stood up when the Bailiff stood up.

"All rise, the 2nd judicial district for the City and County of Denver in the State of Colorado, Appellate Court, Division X, is now in session. The Honorable Judge Donna Pinewood, presiding, over the case of *Cecilia Duffy-Downs Et. Al. V. The State of Colorado.* Case number 20AP7719."

"You may be seated," she said, sitting down. Daniel looked at her ghastly white face and knew something was terribly wrong.

"Mr. Fargo, you may begin with your opening statement."

Mr. Fargo stood up, gathered one piece of paper which contained his opening statement and cleared his throat before speaking.

"Good morning, Your Honor. The State's case against the appealers will show that the State followed proper courtroom protocol and at no time were the appealers rights violated in any manner. This is simply a waste of tax payers' money and the court's time; thank you, Your Honor," said Kenneth as he sat back down.

Daniel was getting ready to stand up when Cecilia handed him a bumper sticker. He took the bumper sticker and slid it into his briefcase for later viewing.

"So noted; is counsel for the appealers ready with opening statements?"

Daniel stood up and smiled.

"Yes, I am. Good morning, Your Honor, it is good not only to see you again, but to be in your courtroom again."

"Why, thank you, Mr. Marcos. We have had many good, heated debates about civil and criminal law in the past."

"Yes, we have, Your Honor."

"Before you begin your opening statements, this court would like to recognize Attorney Daniel Marcos, Esquire for being nominated as a possible replacement for the retiring chief justice of the state supreme court," she said as everyone started clapping.

"Thank you, again, Your Honor. It was indeed an honor to be considered as a possible replacement by someone with whom I've had a few serious legal tussles in the past."

"You're welcome; now, for your opening statements."

"Thank you, again, Your Honor. Contrary to what my esteemed colleague may have said, there were several violations of my client's rights by both the prosecutor and, unfortunately, the judge, in their respective cases."

He paused before being interrupted by Kenneth.

"Objection, Your Honor, can you prove any of what you're saying?"

"Objection overruled, please continue, Mr. Marcos."

"Thank you, Your Honor, and I certainly intend on trying to do so, Mr. Fargo. My clients, when their respective employers moved them to this state, relinquished their rights, privileges and immunities that you Mr. Fargo, Your Honor, I and millions of other U.S. Citizens/Coloradans take for granted."

"Mr. Marcos, no one, by becoming a citizen of the State of Colorado, relinquishes any of their rights, privileges and immunities which are granted to all U.S. citizens," said Judge Pinewood, whose face had turned from no emotion to one of grave concern.

"Sadly enough, that is exactly what happened in the trial court with the same prosecutor and judge, Your Honor."

Kenneth was about to say something but was interrupted by Donna.

"Name, to this court, any right, or rights, that your clients are alleged to have relinquished when they came to this state."

"Their 5th Amendment right of not having to bear witness against yourself in a court of law, is one. They also relinquished their 14th Amendment, Section 1, protections."

"Objection, Your Honor, this line of speech is irrelevant to this case. I reviewed the trial court's proceedings and found no evidence of such an allegation," said Ken, standing up and remaining that way.

"Can you really prove this, Mr. Marcos?"

"Yes, I believe that I can make and articulate the case for such allegations."

"Objection overruled."

"Thank you, Your Honor. Up until my clients were arrested and charged with Domestic Violence against each other, my clients were second class citizens in this state; ghosts in the eyes of the law, if you want to call them such."

"Objection, Your Honor, his clients look pretty real to me," Ken said as he looked over the couples and their kids.

"I must admit, Mr. Marcos, Mr. Fargo is right; they look real to me as well," said Donna, who was now starting to sweat.

"In the physical sense, yes, my clients are real. However, in the State of Colorado, under the criminal statute that they were arrested for, charged with and convicted of, they are ghosts; they don't exist."

"Your Honor, I must object to this line of speech once again," said Ken.

"Mr. Marcos, would you please explain to this court, in terms that it understands, what you're talking about!" she snapped.

"I was hoping to avoid doing that, Your Honor, because I can't clearly speak of what is at the heart of this whole, judicial travesty, without being disbarred."

"I understand you've been handicapped; please try and do your best."

"I will certainly try, Your Honor. All right; my clients were arrested, charged with and convicted of violating Colorado Revised Statutes, Title 18, Article 6, Part 800.3, Domestic Violence. The Domestic Violence statute has a two-prong test that must be passed, just like there is a two-prong test for Miranda Rights being read to a suspect. In other words, without one you cannot have the other."

"Then, what part of this two-prong test did your clients fail?" asked Donna.

"The intimate relationship part of the statute; in the eyes of Colorado law, my clients intimate relationships and those similarly situated, does not exist. The trial court erred, Your Honor and in so doing, committed several major offenses."

"Objection, Your Honor, his statements have no grounds."

"Objection sustained."

"Your Honor, the trial court erred when it asked my clients about their intimate relationships. In so doing, whether intentional or not, the prosecutor violated Article II, Section 31 of the Colorado State Constitution and also violated Colorado Revised Statutes Title 14, Article 2, Part 104, Section 1, Paragraph B."

Daniel paused, waiting until the judge was through making her notes on the case.

"Remember, my clients and those similarly situated, waived their right not to have to bear witness against themselves or their mate for their crimes except under certain circumstances. My clients didn't want to commit perjury while on the witness stand, but again they had no other choice."

"Prove it, Mr. Marcos," said Ken, hoping that Daniel would say the words he was told to listen for by Rick Sanchez.

"Your Honor, if you review the court transcripts of case number 20CR1999 and look at pages three hundred sixty-five through three hundred sixty-nine, along with case number 20CR2000 and look at pages four hundred and four through four hundred nine, and please review case number 20CR2001 and look at pages three hundred ninety-nine through four hundred and one."

Daniel saw Donna going through the transcripts.

"Mr. Marcos, the prosecutor asked them if they were married; what is wrong with using that line of questioning to establish the intimate relationship part of the crime?" asked Donna, almost fearful of the answer.

"That is where the trial court erred, Your Honor. My clients intimate relationships and also of those that are similarly situated are not valid or recognized in this state. Therefore, the crime they were charged with can't exist without the primary prong of the two prongs."

"Well, then, what should your clients have been charged with?" asked Ken, with a certain amount of sarcasm in his voice.

"Third Degree Assault and even that one could be reduced to something else. I would possibly argue for no jail time in exchange for a fine and some community service work."

"Objection, Your Honor, doesn't the state supreme court case of *People V. Disher,* 224 P.3d pages 254 through 258 apply in this case?" asked Ken.

"No, Mr. Fargo, that case doesn't apply here for several reasons," replied Daniel, before the judge could answer.

"Mr. Marcos, are you trying to tell this court that your clients and those similarly situated, to use your own words, have . . . ."

"Don't say it, Your Honor," said Daniel, sternly.

"This is my courtroom, Mr. Marcos, and I can say whatever I want or need to say."

"No, Your Honor, because if you do, I am reasonably certain that one of Mr. Sanchez's cronies will have you either censured or impeached for saying the words."

"I see, Mr. Marcos; do you have anything else for this court to consider before I render my decision?"

"Yes, Your Honor, does this court, or any court in the State of Colorado, have the authority to downgrade my clients' and those similarly situated, intimate relationships to the level of Designated Beneficiaries Agreement, as defined by Title 15, Article 22 of Colorado Revised Statutes?"

"I will take it under consideration and we will take a ten minute recess while I make a decision," she said, banging down her gavel two times before leaving her courtroom.

"All rise," said Sandy.

Court reconvened ten minutes later and Judge Pinewood looked worse than before.

"All rise, the 2nd judicial district for the City and County of Denver in the State of Colorado, Appellate Court, Division X, is now in session. The Honorable Judge Donna Pinewood, presiding, over the case of *Cecilia Duffy-Downs Et. Al. V. The State of Colorado.* Case number 20AP7719."

"You may be seated. After reviewing the evidence presented in this appeals case and since the appealer's attorney has been hampered by outside forces beyond his control, I find that I must uphold the lower court's decision. However, as to the question that the appealer's attorney asked in open court, this court could not find anything giving any court in this state the authority to downgrade what your clients and those similarly situated have in reference to an intimate relationship."

She paused before continuing.

"Does the State of Colorado wish to appeal this court's ruling?"

Ken stood up, smiling confidently.

"No, Your Honor," he said, sitting back down.

"So noted; does the appealer's attorney wish to appeal this court's ruling?"

Daniel stood up, after having conferred with his clients.

"We do, Your Honor. At this time, I am aware that this normally involves a three judge panel. My clients and I wish to waive said three judge panel hearing and invoke Appellate Court Rule 113, Section D."

"So noted; this case is hereby passed to the next step in the appeals process. Let the court records show that the appealer's attorney has invoked Appellate Court Rule 113, Section D," she said, banging down her gavel two times again.

"All rise," said Sandy.

Daniel left for the airport right away so he could get home that night on the last flight of the day from the Denver International Airport.

CHAPTER 6

The newest chief judge of the 10th Federal Circuit Court was coming up in the elevator to the 4th floor of the courthouse building to his chambers. His chambers were room four hundred fifty-five while his courtroom was room four hundred fifty-four. He stepped out of the elevator and walked a short distance down the hallway to his clerk's office. He opened the door to his clerk's office and walked inside.

Chief Judge Ulysses Lyle Sorensen was a huge hulking man, standing six feet eight inches tall, weighing in at over three hundred pounds. He was broad shouldered and walked with purposeful strides. He also possessed a deep, booming voice whenever he spoke. He was an American Eskimo by ethnicity, but you almost couldn't tell by the dark, tan-looking skin he possessed from his father's side of the family, an Aztec Indian from Mexico. He kept his black hair as short as possible so he could maintain his professional look at all times.

He saw the stack of case files sitting in his inbox and took them into his chambers, closing the door behind himself. Chief Judge Sorensen finally reached the bottom of the stack about two hours later. The last case read just like a joke to him so he read the case file twice. After the second reading, he smiled as he closed the case file.

"*Really? Seriously? This has to be a joke, no one really did this,*" he thought as he exited his chambers and put the case files on his clerk's desktop. His clerk was busy typing away on the computer.

"Pretty funny joke to play on the new chief judge with that case file on top; I know, I've been initiated and accepted into the clan."

His clerk took the top case file off the stack, opened it up, looked over the case file briefing, and put it back on the top of the stack.

"That's no joke, Your Honor."

"What?!"

"The Colorado State Legislature really did it."

"Oh, you've got to be kidding me; okay, then, why did I get the case?"

"Retiring Senior Chief Judge Rowland Allen thought this would be right up your alley since you're the best judge this bench has seen in a long time on Constitutional Law matters."

"I still think it's a joke; I mean, that case file is what impeachment hearings are made of."

"The truth is stranger than fiction, Your Honor."

"I believe Mark Twain said that based on the observation that fiction has to follow a certain prescribed course whereas the truth does not. Very well, put that case on my docket for January 6th, 2021."

"Yes, Your Honor," he said as he opened up the judge's court docket for that day. He looked over the time slots that were available and found two that would work for the judge.

"You have 10:45 a.m. or 1:00 p.m. available to hear that case."

"10:45 a.m. will work for me, and fill out subpoenas for both of the state Senators mentioned in that case. I would like to see their voting records as well."

"Yes, Your Honor."

Rick was looking across the table at a dear friend at a local restaurant close to the courthouse. Judge Bach was visibly nervous while he ate lunch with Rick. He finished off his bowl of chili before using the napkin to wipe his face.

"So, Your Honor, Attorney Daniel Marcos has forgone the three judge panel and pressed forward to the state Supreme Court?" asked Rick.

"Yes, from what I read of Judge Pinewood's opinion, he invoked Appellate Court Rule 113, Section D. Is there any way that the state Supreme Court will rule in his client's favor?"

"No, those Senate bills will insure that that state Supreme Court remains crippled."

"There's no way?" asked Judge Bach, nervously, once again looking for reassurance from Rick.

"No way, unless someone hires an attorney that would ask for a Federal Circuit Court order against enforcement of those Senate bills. What is my legal advisor doing here?" asked Rick as he stood up and walked over to where she was.

"Yes, Dianne, what is it?" asked Rick, rather irritated.

"I just received a call from the Colorado State Legislature's Office of The Honorable James Miles Legislative Law Library. She said that a Chief Judge Ulysses Lyle Sorensen of the 10th Federal Circuit Court served her with subpoenas asking for copies of those Senate bills you told me to be on the alert for. Also, she was served with another subpoena asking for the voting records of certain state Senators," she said, watching with pleasure the angst on Rick's face.

"Thank you, and I will see you back at the office."

Rick returned to the table and Judge Bach could tell something was very wrong.

"Is everything okay, Rick?" he asked, politely.

"Yes, why should it not be?!" snapped Rick.

"Just asking."

"Sorry, Your Honor; here let me take care of the bill," said Rick, dropping several $20.00 bills on the table top as he left; Judge Bach returned to his courtroom still thinking about what happened at lunch.

Daniel had looked over the marriage license thoroughly for about two weeks along with the bumper sticker that Cecilia had obtained for him. It was a Saturday afternoon when Daniel's personal cell phone started ringing. He set the bumper sticker and the marriage license down on the tabletop in the kitchen to answer the call.

"Hello?"

"Daniel, it's your answering service, I have a Judge Donna Pinewood on the phone for you."

"Yes, please put Her Honor through."

There was an audible click on the line.

"Hello, Daniel and I wanted you to be the first one to know that I am quitting the bench."

"Why, Your Honor?"

"Your case and all of those similarly situated has shown me the hate and animosity on the bench directed at those types of people; I can't take it anymore."

"They say that judges don't have a conscience, but it appears that you have one, Your Honor. Are you going into private practice, then?"

"I don't know; you have a very long and rough road ahead of you, Daniel."

"I am well aware of that, Your Honor; don't quit the bench on account of my clients. You did your job. Don't apologize for doing it."

"Daniel, you and I took an oath when we became attorneys. Part of that oath says we wouldn't let personal feelings cloud the issues. I can't sit on the bench anymore knowing that your clients aren't treated equally in the eyes of Colorado law. It's all about whom they fell in love with and married. The word marriage is what all of this hate is about."

"You're very perceptive, Your Honor. May I suggest that you help out one of the groups here in the state that is trying to put an end to all of that hate and animosity?"

"I'll think about it, Daniel, and good luck with the state Supreme Court. You have two justices that outright hate you, your clients and those similarly situated."

"Let me guess, Associate Justices Regina Tartik and Caroline Hayes?"

"Yes, and from a woman's point of view, Associate Justice Tartik is a really big bitch."

"Thank you for the heads up on her."

"Chief Justice Wisenrock, Associate Justice Vince Kartheny and Darcy Smith are on your side for you. I believe Associate Justice Kartheny has a gay son who lives in Washington, D.C."

"That might be useful when the time comes; what about Associate Justices Carson Robins and Blanca Hale?"

"They are neutral and thankfully don't buy into too many things."

"Well, looks like I have some serious convincing to do when I get there."

"Yes."

"Are Associate Justices Tartik and Hayes from either the El Paso County or some of the northern county areas?"

"Associate Justice Tartik is a Colorado Springs native. Associate Justice Hayes is from the Loveland or Greeley area, I think."

"Great, goodbye," he said, hanging up the phone.

"Goodbye, Daniel," she said, hanging up the phone.

Daniel went upstairs to his small office and checked his email. There were the usual hate emails, then his regular emails. One of the last emails was from Leslie. It contained another cryptic message: "Good morning, Skipper, maintain course and speed towards the Promised Land. Two battleships have engaged the enemy and will keep them busy until they run out of ammunition, XO." Daniel replied to the email and then saw the last email.

The subject line said, "Appeals Case 20AP7719." He opened up the email and read the email in its entirety. The case had been put on the state Supreme Court's 2020-2021 docket session. The date had not been set yet, but at least Daniel's request for the court of last resort in the state had not fallen on deaf ears. He turned off his computer and was about to go downstairs to fix everyone breakfast when Chayton wandered into the room.

"Good morning, Dad," he said, rubbing his eyes.

"Good morning, Sunshine, and I have something to show you after we eat," said Daniel, picking him up and taking him downstairs.

After breakfast was finished and Daniel washed the dishes, he went upstairs to his small office and opened up his briefcase. He withdrew the envelope and closed it back up. Daniel called Todd, Shilah and Chayton all together in the family room downstairs. He handed the marriage license around to everyone so they could see it for themselves.

"So that there will be no secrets of any kind in this family, that is the reason why we weren't invited to Seth's wedding," said Daniel, choking slightly.

"He did marry another boy," said Chayton, handing the license back to Daniel.

"Yes, it would appear he did, Chayton," said Daniel, handing the license to Shilah for him to look at one more time.

"Daniel, that marriage license doesn't say it's a same-sex marriage license," said Shilah.

"You're right, but if you look at the space where it asks for the bride and groom's names, you will find two extra spaces. They are labeled bride A and bride B or groom A and groom B."

"I must have been misled in law school, Daniel, because I fully expected it to say same-sex marriage license on it," said Shilah, handing the license back to Daniel.

"Dad, how can he not like girls?" asked Todd, trying to stifle tears and looking confused.

"The best evidence from the medical community from the past forty years seems to indicate he was born that way, Todd. As the years went on, he liked boys more and more."

"So, it's not a choice?"

"No, that's correct. If it were a choice, then simply giving him a pill or something for him to like girls would be easy. I want you to remember something; he is still your brother, and he loves you all very much."

"Then, why doesn't he come to visit us?" asked Todd, haughtily.

"Because, he knows, in this state, his marriage is not valid or recognized. If something were to happen to him, his husband or the twin boys they have, there would be no recourse in many matters. Matters which everyone in this room takes for granted."

"Okay, I'm a little confused now, Daniel. If Seth is gay, how did he have kids?" asked Todd, feeling a little stupid now.

"I think it stems from a nasty little incident about four years ago when he and Tyler had an ugly fight over something. They both went out with some ladies they worked with and got drunk; do I need to paint a picture for you?"

"No, I think I can figure it out for myself," said Todd.

"Good; I had to do some adoption paperwork a few years ago because the women were killed during a hurricane that hit the island. The island government was not grateful to Seth or Tyler for wanting to adopt the kids. They felt that the dolphin preserve in the Caribbean wasn't a good place to raise a family. The government additionally felt that two males raising kids would make the kids predisposed to becoming gay themselves. So far, it hasn't happened."

"What stopped the government from sending the kids somewhere else?" asked Shilah.

"The day that Seth and Tyler filed their custody paperwork with the country that has jurisdiction down there, that country became the 24th country to recognize and abide by same-sex marriages, civil unions, domestic partnerships or whatever other legal status is given to same-sex couples by their respective countries. This allowed Seth and Tyler to complete the adoption process as the country made them equal in the eyes of the law to include benefits such as adoption rights."

"Can we go visit Seth sometime?" asked Chayton.

"We will, next year, when this appeals case is over, I promise."

"Okay, Dad."

After everyone had left the room, he went upstairs to his bedroom to talk to Shilah.

"Shilah, I'm going to need your help now, more than ever. I need you to get all the information, good, bad or indifferent on this issue of same-sex marriages and same-sex relationships."

"I already have, Daniel. All ten of the fifty gigabyte, Blu-ray discs are at the office in the safe."

"Thank you," said Daniel as they left the bedroom together and ran right into a news reporter. Chayton was yelling at Daniel as both Daniel and Shilah took up defensive postures. This caused the reporter to drop what she was carrying on the floor and scream. Shilah slipped up behind her and grabbed her arms with a grip of steel.

"Who the hell are you and how did you get into my house?!" barked Daniel as he leaned into the bedroom a little, tapping the side of the dresser next to the door with his fingers. The little drawer opened on the side of the dresser and he retrieved his Glock model 20® with a 25-round magazine sticking out the bottom. He then pointed it at her head.

"I'm Nancy from the *Daily Sentinel* newspaper in Grand Junction and when I arrived, the door was partially open. I knocked on the door and no one answered," she squeaked as Shilah lifted her off the floor a little bit.

"You know you could have gotten yourself killed for doing what you just did," said Daniel.

"I know it fully well now; please don't shoot me. I thought Mary from the *Ironton Gazette* had said something to you about my stopping by to interview you," she squeaked again.

"Well, I do believe she did say something to me about your stopping by; terribly sorry about the misunderstanding, Nancy; Shilah you can let her go now."

Shilah lowered her to the floor and went downstairs. While Daniel put his gun back up into the special safe, Nancy massaged her arms while picking up her things.

"If you will please follow me downstairs to my office, we can talk there," said Daniel, pointing the way.

When they arrived downstairs, Nancy had a chance to meet Todd and Chayton. She was shown to the small office where Daniel closed the door so that she could begin the interview with privacy.

"Is the man who grabbed me and lifted me off the floor Shilah Haynes, by any chance?" she asked.

"Yes," said Daniel, smiling.

"I thought he was going to break my arms."

"He probably would have."

"I'm thankful that he didn't. Mary told me that you don't like reporters."

"She's right, because reporters don't print the truth anymore. The truth doesn't sell much newspaper space, airtime or internet site space."

"I give you my word that what you say will be printed in the Sunday edition of the *Daily Sentinel.* I will make sure that you receive a copy of it."

"Very well, what questions do you want me to answer?"

"Do you and Shilah sleep together?"

"Yes, is there a problem with that sleeping arrangement?"

"Well, someone could construe that you are possibly gay, with that type of sleeping arrangement. Someone could also construe that you might have sympathy towards your clients and those similarly situated, to use your own words. Besides, you're a very attractive man; you could play both sides of the street, if you know what I mean," she said, writing furiously.

"Are you asking me what my actual sexual orientation is? That could be interpreted as an illegal question."

"No, nothing like that; why do you two sleep together?" she asked, still a little flustered.

"Because the basement downstairs needs to be inspected by the building inspector before Shilah can sleep down there; the building inspector is in Durango and doesn't come up here to Ironton until there is less than three feet of snow on the ground. That means he won't be up here until sometime in late May or early June."

"I see, and were you aware that you have a campaign office in Denver?"

"No, I was not aware of that. Who is manning this alleged office?"

"A group of volunteers from the LGBTQ community in Denver are manning the office. Do you think you can be selected or elected to the position of the chief justice of the Colorado State Supreme Court?"

"Since I have no political ambitions, I wouldn't stand a chance against my competitors."

"But, by not having any political ambitions, wouldn't that make you the perfect candidate for the job? I mean, you couldn't be influenced by campaign contributions from special interest groups."

"Yes, I suppose it would seem to make me a better candidate than my competitors."

"There have been rumors in the press over the last twenty years or so that people in the LGBTQ community want to legalize prostitution, pedophilia, polygamy/bigamy, etc. Is there any truth to those rumors?"

"None; let me give you the answer to the prostitution part of your question first, then we will move on to the other issues. Let me know when you are ready?"

She pulled out a digital recorder and set it up for the answer.

"I'm ready now."

"The only state that ever legalized prostitution was Nevada. The taxes gathered off of prostitution earnings are the number one source of revenue for the state next to the taxes collected on gambling winnings. That state, in order to legalize prostitution, had to add a whole section to their revenue codes which necessitated the creation of a special tax stamp, tax payer ID, etc."

He paused before continuing.

"Next, the Department of Public Health and the Environment, or whatever it is called in that state, had to create special health guidelines for the men and women who work in that state in that industry. They have to carry special health cards with them at all times; health screens are performed regularly, and they have to file income taxes on the money they make. I know that you doubt me, so look it up for yourself. This information is a matter of public record."

"You mean to tell me that all of those hookers, whether they are men or women, have to carry health cards on them and have to have tax payer ID numbers?"

"Yes, the tax payer ID numbers are usually given to the madams for the men and women who work for them. If they contract some sort of STD during their employment, they are forbidden, by law, from doing their job until the STD is cleared up. Sometimes, they have to be medically retired from their job because of the STD. Remember, even in that state, prostitution is still a crime in five counties which includes the city of Las Vegas."

"What about legalizing pedophilia?"

"My clients and those similarly situated, generally speaking, in the LGBTQ community, oppose the legalization of pedophilia in any form. They further demand that laws punishing such behavior be as harsh as possible. They demand that law enforcement do its job by catching and punishing those people who break the law. The same goes for bestiality."

"I never mentioned anything about bestiality."

"You put it on your list along with other crimes."

"What about the legalization of polygamy/bigamy?"

"All states joining the Union following the Civil War, after the ratification of the 14th Amendment and before their statehood would be granted for admittance to the Union, had to have polygamy/bigamy identified in their respective state constitutions as a crime punishable by imprisonment and fines. In other words, these crimes would never be able to be legalized without the prospect of losing statehood."

"It seems I have been lied to by my own colleagues."

"So it would appear, by the look on your face when I answered the questions truthfully. If you don't believe me, you can look it up for yourself; again, it is a matter of public record."

"I might just do that; there are rumors that your clients are pro-choice."

"You've been lied to once again. My clients and those similarly situated are pro-life, generally speaking."

"Do you see your appeals case going to the U.S. Supreme Court?"

"No, it won't go that far."

"Are you so sure?"

"In order for my appeals case to get that far, I would have to raise some very serious and ugly constitutional law questions in open court that would put the final disposition of the case beyond the authority and jurisdiction of the Colorado State Supreme Court."

"How so?"

"In accordance with Article III, Section 2 of the U.S. Constitution, the U.S. Supreme Court shall have original jurisdiction in cases arising out of conflicts of federal constitutional law and state constitutional laws. If you don't believe me, you can look it up for yourself."

"I just might do that, Mr. Marcos. There are rumors that your clients are child molesters and don't deserve any legal protections."

"Again, you've been lied to by your friends in the mainstream media; that rumor isn't true. If you want proof, look at the Belfour Study done right here in this state in 2017; the findings were published in 2018. I think it will open your eyes on this issue."

"I will check that out as well. Do you believe that the voter-passed initiative that became the Defense of Marriage Act is unconstitutional?"

"I will not directly answer that question, but I will answer that question if asked in a court of law. To find the answer, you should look at the Preamble to the Colorado State Constitution, then look at Article II, Sections 29 and 31 of the Colorado State constitution, and finally look at Colorado Revised Statutes, Title 14."

"I think I will. Do you believe that those who are married, whether that marriage is traditional or same-sex, should have their rights defended in or by a court of law?"

"Absolutely and the U.S. Supreme Court has ruled fourteen times over the last 100 plus year journey that a marriage is to be defended by the courts, against unfair and unconstitutional laws."

"Do you mean miscegenation laws?"

"Yes, the landmark U.S. Supreme Court cases of *Loving V. Virginia*, 388 U.S. 1, 1967 followed by the *Turner V. Safely* 482 U.S. 78, 1987. I am happy to report that Colorado eliminated its miscegenation laws in 1957 with no ill effects to the role of marriage."

"I've heard of the Loving case, but not the other one. Can you tell me a little about that one?"

"The Turner V. Safley case dealt with an inmate that wanted to get married in the Missouri penal system. Missouri penal law wouldn't allow such a thing unless it was under extreme circumstances. Inmate Turner filed a lawsuit in federal court seeking the right to marry. The U.S. Supreme Court ruled that even if the prison system doesn't allow overnight visits for inmates, the Missouri penal system cannot deny the marriage based on that issue."

"It sounds as though the marriage was defended by the U.S. Supreme Court even though they couldn't consummate the marriage?"

"That's right."

"I see; I heard and read about the Proposition 8 trial in California; could that happen here under the right circumstances?"

"No, the Proposition 8 trial in California occurred because the State of California, in 1995, following Israel's lead, implemented the toughest and only anti-discrimination laws in the U.S. The State of California called it the Unruh Civil Rights Act, Subsection 51, California Revised Statutes Civil Code, Section 10620."

"I didn't know that; looks like I have a lot of research to do for some exclusive articles. I must be going; deadlines you know."

"I know."

She left quickly as Daniel prepared everyone's lunch. When late afternoon approached, Seth, Tyler and the twins called Chayton on the video conference phone he had attached to his computer. Daniel was careful to set it up and take it down each Saturday afternoon, locking it up in the safe downstairs. On this particular Saturday afternoon, Daniel waited until Chayton was done talking to them, before entering into the camera's viewing range; Chayton had left the room just like Daniel had told him to do earlier that morning.

"Seth and Tyler, I need to speak to you privately and seriously," said Daniel.

CHAPTER 7

After Daniel had said Merry Christmas and Happy New Year to Seth, Tyler and the twins, he said goodbye. Seth broke down into tears as he looked into Tyler's eyes before speaking.

"How could someone be so cruel?" sobbed Seth.

"Our marriage license is a matter of public record, Seth."

There was a bright flash of light followed by thunder close by. The early evening thunderstorms were once again rolling onto the tiny island they called home. The tropical air was getting scented with moisture from the falling rain that had yet to reach the ground. A slight breeze was blowing, but it never seemed to cool things down much.

"Seth, Daniel is not only fighting for his clients, he's fighting for everyone else like them in the State of Colorado. He's also fighting for us and our children and grandchildren. How can we not be there when it is US that he needs the most? Besides, I think he deserves to see his grandchildren at least once before he dies, don't you? And how about Chayton, don't you think he wants to see his nephews?"

"I guess you're right, but that state has a despicable, deplorable, racist, discriminatory law where one love for all with no exceptions, doesn't apply."

"I understand, Seth, and I think you pretty much hit all the highlights of that law. I only hope that Daniel will tell us when the court date is, so that we can be there in time."

"I hope so, too. I also found out, through an unnamed news source, that Daniel was on the nomination list that the out going chief justice submitted to the governor a few months ago."

"For what position?"

"The chief justice of the Colorado State Supreme Court."

"Then we definitely should be there."

"Agreed."

The year 2021 had arrived in Silverton, Colorado. There was a large fireworks display outside of city hall, New Year's resolutions were made and songs were sung. Todd had been at a chaperoned party at his girlfriend's house. Daniel had also been invited to go along with Chayton and Shilah. It was about 3:00 a.m. when they all returned home that Saturday morning. Daniel put Chayton to bed and heard Todd get into a shower. Daniel undressed in the dark before getting into bed himself. To Daniel, it seemed as if he had just closed his eyes, when his personal cell phone started ringing. He looked over at the clock; 1:00 p.m.

"Hello?"

"Mr. Marcos, this is Lyle Smith, why are you asking for my son to be prosecuted?"

"Mr. Smith, your son is a juvenile, and you and I know as attorneys that juveniles get off pretty easy."

"It's your name on the victim impact statement."

"Yes, you're right, that is my name on that statement, but it is my insurance company who wants their money back for the damages your son and his friends caused that night. This damage was the result of either you or someone else teaching your son that hate and animosity towards another person because of their actual or perceived sexual orientation or preference is an acceptable family value."

"Your clients aren't acceptable to my family values."

"That's what I thought; goodbye," said Daniel, hanging up the phone and getting out of bed. He found that he was all alone in the house and decided that he should workout downstairs before doing anything else. He worked out, took a shower and then went back downstairs in his bathrobe to wait for everyone to come home.

Monday morning arrived and the afternoon mail had been delivered to the clerks of the various courts within the building that housed the 10th Federal Circuit Court. Chief Judge Sorensen was reviewing his cases for the month of January when his clerk came in with the voting records of the defendants in the case of the Emergency Injunction and Declaratory Relief, case number 21CV0116-ULS. He looked over the voting records and then handed them back to his clerk.

"Make sure those are on my bench when that case comes to my courtroom on Thursday."

"Yes, Your Honor; anything else?"

"No, dismissed."

Daniel opened the mail that had been delivered to the office; there was the usual hate mail; nothing serious yet. He then turned on his computer to check his email from over the long holiday weekend. After sorting through and filing away the hate mail, he saw an email from the clerk of the court for the Colorado State Supreme Court with the date of the hearing. The date of the hearing was May 14th, 2021 which would be the last day of their 2020-2021 sessions and the last session with the current chief justice presiding. Daniel looked at his last email which was from the XO. "Good morning, Skipper, maintain course and speed. Intelligence reports indicate that you should, if you have the time, watch some TV. The randomly selected station will be www. federalcourtstv.gov/10thFederalCircuit/ULS/21CV0116-ULS.htm or TV channel 501; goodbye Skipper." Daniel closed his email, after deleting this one, and turned off his computer.

Thursday morning, January 6th, 2021 had arrived and Chief Judge Ulysses Lyle Sorensen had finally finished off the previous case. Dave Morgan and Della Mortam were setting up their stuff in the courtroom during the break. As the Bailiff readjusted the cameras, State Senators Shelly Reece, representing the 14th State Senate District within Colorado and Debbie Jo Donovan, representing the 26th State Senate District within Colorado, sat nervously next to the attorney they had hired for this case. Dave and Della smiled and waved at them before looking up to the bench. Soon, the front doors of the courtroom opened and the Bailiff stood up as did the rest of the courtroom.

"All rise, the 10th Federal Circuit Court is now in session. The Honorable Chief Judge Ulysses Lyle Sorensen, presiding, over the case of *The State of Colorado V. Della Mortam and Dave Morgan Et. Al.*, case number 21CV0116-ULS."

Ulysses walked up the steps to his bench, sat down, and opened up the case file while his clerk set all of the paperwork down on the bench in front of the judge. The two state Senators looked at each other then started whispering to each other.

"What do you think that stack of paperwork is?" asked Shelly to Debbie Jo.

"I don't know; there was a rumor that this judge had asked for a copy of our voting records for the veto override vote."

"If that is what that stack of paperwork is, then we need to plead no contest to this court action and leave," said Shelly.

"If you decide to leave here to leave me holding the bag, I will make sure that you go down with me," replied Debbie Jo.

Chief Judge Sorensen finally spoke.

"This court will come to order and you may be seated. This is the case of an Emergency Injunction and Declaratory Relief request against the enforcement in whole or in any part of Colorado State Legislature Senate Bills SB15-1155, SB18-1207 and SB19-2701."

He paused before continuing. Daniel had just tuned in from his office via the internet address provided to him.

"These proceedings are being recorded and broadcast in accordance with Federal Circuit Court rules and regulations from the Proposition 8 trail in 2010, www.federalcourtstv. gov/10thFederalCircuit/ULS/21CV0116-ULS.htm, as well as TV Channels 501 and 503. Is the State of Colorado, also known as the defendants in this case, represented in this court for the proceedings?" he asked.

Shelly, Debbie Jo and their attorney stood up.

"We are, Your Honor," they said as they stood together.

"Very well, please state your names and who you work for, for the court records."

"Certainly, Your Honor. I am Jodi Torkelsen of the Law Firm of Kyle, Kyle and Bald. I represent the two state Senators you subpoenaed last year."

"So noted; are the plaintiffs in this case represented in this courtroom?"

Della and Dave stood up as Jodi, Debbie Jo and Shelly sat back down.

"The plaintiffs are represented, Your Honor."

"Very well; please state your names and who you work for or represent, for the court records."

"Certainly, Your Honor. I am Della Mortam and this is Dave Morgan. We represent ourselves from our own private law firms."

"So noted; do you represent only yourselves or do you represent a group of some kind that is in need of this emergency court intervention?"

"Your Honor, we represent a group of at least 605,000 Coloradans who are in desperate need of relief from the enforcement, in whole or in part, of these Senate bills," answered Dave quickly and confidently.

"I see and why aren't any of these people in this courtroom or protesting outside the courthouse, or something like that?"

"Your Honor, they feel that the court holds hate and animosity against them for who they are. They also feel that the court will not do its job because of who they are," replied Dave.

"I see and are you doing this case pro bono?"

"Yes, Your Honor, we are," replied Della as she stood up and Dave sat back down.

"So noted; before we begin formally, this court states that it holds no hate or animosity towards any person or group; this court wishes this to be clearly understood by your clients, Della Mortam and Dave Morgan."

"What you said is clear, Your Honor, and will be passed along as such," said Della, carefully choosing her words so as to not give away that she was getting more and more nervous being in the courtroom.

"Thank you, Ms. Mortam. The plaintiffs may begin their side of the case, and I will allow twenty-five minutes for both sides to try and convince this court that their side is right; you may begin now," said Ulysses as he set the time on a small timer he kept at his bench.

Della took a few deep breaths and began speaking.

"Good morning, Your Honor, and, if it pleases the court, my colleague and I, who represent a severely disadvantaged group of

Colorado citizens, request that this court render the enforcement, in whole or in part, of Senate bills SB15-1155, SB18-1207 and SB19-2701 to be effective immediately."

She paused while she shuffled her note cards around.

"This court, Your Honor, has jurisdiction over this case in accordance with Title 28, United States Code, As Amended, Sections 1331 and 1343 apply."

She paused once again before continuing.

"These Senate bills are insidious and unconstitutional in that they cripple the Colorado State Supreme Court from doing its job properly, correctly and legally as intended by the Colorado Constitution. These Senate bills are a direct result of the legislature in trying to prevent the court of last resort in the state from being able to uphold one of its most sacred duties to defend those who cannot defend themselves in a court of law because they are highly disadvantaged."

She paused again; this time the stress and anxiety had started to lessen.

"The first Senate bill is clearly unconstitutional because the only purpose for having that law in place is to prevent the court from upholding another sacred duty by determining the constitutionality of a state law or an amendment to the state's constitution in a given set of circumstances."

"What makes Senate Bill SB15-1155 so unconstitutional?" asked Ulysses as Dave stood up to help Della out.

"Your Honor, Senate Bill SB15-1155 violates both the due process and equal protection clauses of the 14th Amendment of the U.S. Constitution. It also violates the 11th Amendment. Since the Colorado State Supreme Court, herein after referred to as the CSSC, can no longer invalidate a state law or amendment to the state constitution, except under extremely grave circumstances, the law is unconstitutional," he said as he sat down and Della stood back up to complete the answer for Dave.

"Your Honor, the group of Coloradans we represent and those similarly situated in this state, cannot receive, nor can they expect to receive, equal protection under the law with the Senate bill active. This Senate bill serves no other purpose except to prevent and/or stop the CSSC from doing the job of upholding the laws of the state except under extreme circumstances such as breach of the peace, rioting and insurrections or other types of civil unrest which is completely uncalled for by the legislature."

"Very well; please go on."

Dave stood up to address the court once again, shuffling around his note cards just as Della had done earlier.

"Your Honor, Senate Bill SB18-1207 is in direct violation of both the due process and equal protection clauses of the 14th Amendment. This Senate bill provides for exemptions to Home Rule cities being immune from the decisions and opinions of the CSSC if it is contrary to their city or county ordinances. In other words, this Senate bill allows Home Rule cities to be outside the jurisdiction of the CSSC. The only purpose of this Senate bill was to further cripple the CSSC in performing its duty."

Dave paused before continuing.

"The Colorado State Constitution, when it was originally written in 1876, clearly stated that the state shall have a supreme court and that the CSSC will have original jurisdiction within the state on matters of state law or conflicts between state law and city or county ordinances. This Senate bill does nothing more than provide for a protected class of citizens within certain cities that are out of the jurisdiction of the CSSC's opinions and decisions. This clearly violates Article III of the Colorado Constitution."

"Just a minute, before you go on, how many Home Rule cities are there currently in the State of Colorado?" asked Ulysses.

"I am not sure of the exact number, Your Honor, but it exceeds twenty-five," said Della, quickly, as she stood up.

"Okay, and I suppose Denver is one of those Home Rule cities?"

"Yes, Your Honor, you're correct," said Della as she sat back down.

Dave sat down and Della stood back up with a fresh set of note cards in her left hand to complete the opening statement.

"Your Honor, Senate Bill SB19-2701 has no other purpose than to further isolate, condemn and show hate, animosity and cruel treatment to those who are different in some ways than you, I and my colleagues here in this courtroom. The CSSC should have their proper rights and powers restored to them in order that they can do their job properly, legally and correctly, as intended by Article III of the Colorado Constitution. This Senate bill shows the utmost contempt for the courts and shows how much hate and animosity the legislature has for our three-part system of government. The legislature has shown that it wants to have some sort of ultimate power and further wishes to show that the CSSC has no teeth; thank you, Your Honor," she said, sitting back down.

"Let me ask you some questions to clarify some things about your request for this emergency injunction. Did the governor or governors veto these bills?"

Della stood up.

"Yes, Your Honor, both Governors Smith and Garcia vetoed these bills. They were sent back to the full legislature where they were overridden with more than the required 66% vote. This vote was spearheaded by the defendants in this case, Your Honor."

"Did the Colorado State Attorney General object in any way to these Senate bills?"

"Yes, Your Honor and when they were in their respective judiciary committees in both the House and the Senate, they were amended prior to their passage," said Della, starting to get worried again.

"Very well, can you sum up the request again for this court as to why you and your clients and those similarly situated, need this emergency injunction?"

Dave stood up. "Your Honor, there is a very important appeals case that is slated for argument in the CSSC's courtroom over a particular criminal law statute and the constitutionality of Article II, Section 31 of the Colorado State Constitution, which was enacted by voter referendum in 2006, I believe. Without the emergency injunction to prevent the enforcement, in whole or in part, of these Senate bills, the appealers in the case, the people we represent, and the CSSC cannot expect to receive a fair and just outcome," said Dave as he sat back down.

"So noted; and, I must say, well argued in this court. I think that this case is a little premature, but since the decision probably won't be released until during or after the appeals case goes to the CSSC, I understand why you think the people you represent and those similarly situated need the emergency injunction."

"Thank you, Your Honor," said Della.

"Do you believe those you represent and those similarly situated are politically powerless in the State of Colorado?"

"Yes, Your Honor, they are politically powerless. They have representation in the legislature, but no real power in that representation," answered Della, getting worried again.

"In other words, their representation in the legislature is akin to a token or ceremonious position?" asked Ulysses, trying to see the picture that Della and Dave had tried to paint for him.

"Yes, Your Honor," replied Della.

"If the people that you and your colleague represent in this court are so politically powerless and disadvantaged, why didn't those same people have you file a Title 42, United States Code as Amended, Section 1983 lawsuit?"

"Your Honor, the people we represent could have done just that. They're keenly aware of the fact that State of Colorado's government retained lawyers have an unlimited war chest of money to draw from. Whereas the people we represent, do not have an unlimited chest of money to fight the government appointed lawyers."

Della paused before she finished off what she was saying.

"I would like the court to take judicial notice of the fact that government appointed lawyers are famous for getting multiple continuances, and making the other party go blind with paperwork. The people we represent wish to go this route, instead, before resorting to the one you mentioned, Your Honor."

"Having been in court cases with government appointed lawyers for several Title 42, U.S.C. Section 1983 cases, I can sympathize with your clientele," said Ulysses smiling; the whole courtroom chuckled, including Daniel in his office.

Judge Sorensen was quiet before asking another question.

"Has your clientele tried to bring out subtle changes in the law that would bend the law more in their favor?"

"Yes, Your Honor, they have tried since 2009. They finally gave up in 2019," replied Dave, now standing beside Della, trying to show his support for her.

"I see and do you have any explanation for this giving up of the battle?"

"Simple, Your Honor, their efforts, despite being very gallant, were falling on deaf ears," replied Dave, flatly.

"That makes sense; thank you. Defendants, you may begin your opening statements to the court after the court takes a ten minute recess," he said, standing up, closing the case file up and banging down his gavel.

"All rise," said the Bailiff.

About fifteen minutes later, Judge Sorensen returned to his courtroom. When the Bailiff stood up, so did everyone else.

"All rise, the 10th Federal Circuit Court is now in session. The Honorable Chief Judge Ulysses Lyle Sorensen, presiding, over the case of *The State of Colorado V. Della Mortam and Dave Morgan Et. Al.*, case number 21CV0116-ULS."

Ulysses walked up to his bench, sat down and opened up the case file once again.

"You may be seated and this court will come to order. The defendants may begin their side of the case."

Their lawyer stood up.

"Good morning, Your Honor and if it pleases the court, I represent the defendants in this case. You subpoenaed my clients late last year and they have come to your court to argue for their side of the case."

She paused before continuing.

"I wish to remind the court and the plaintiffs in this case that they bear a heavy burden of proof to prove their side of the argument. Simply put, Your Honor, they have no such proof. My clients did not violate any known laws or any known constitutional amendments. My clients feel that the court is wasting its time as well as my client's and my time on a wild goose chase."

She paused once again.

"Contrary to what the plaintiffs said, these laws are just and not unconstitutional in any manner."

"Hold up right there; let's look at Senate Bill SB15-1155, the short title is the Colorado State Supreme Court Cannot Legislate from the Bench. Have you or your clients ever thought that maybe the legislature passes laws that are contrary to either the state or the federal constitutions?" asked Ulysses, while paying special attention to the lawyer's facial features. He was looking for something that could be useful later on, and he found it when she furled her eyebrows a little bit.

"Your Honor, the whole purpose of that Senate bill was to prevent activist judges from either legislating or telling the state legislature how to do its job on writing or passing laws for the state," she answered, haughtily; that's what the judge wanted to hear.

"Have you or your clients ever considered that it is sometimes the job; no, let me rephrase that, it is the duty of a state supreme court, to determine the constitutionality of the laws or voter referendums that come before it when challenged properly by the citizenry?"

She turned to speak for a few seconds with the Senators.

"Your Honor, my clients do concede that the court does sometimes have to do such things in or under certain circumstances. However, judges shouldn't tell the legislature what to do or how to do it all the time."

"Okay, that seems to me to be a weak response, but we need to move on as time is short. Let's move on to Senate Bill SB18-1207; briefly, Home Rule Cities are immune from Colorado State Supreme Court opinions or decisions if they are contrary to the Home Rule Cities laws or something to that effect."

"Yes, Your Honor," she replied, flatly.

"That Senate bill seems to direct animosity towards the Colorado State Supreme Court, stating that Home Rule Cities are exempt or immune from the very court decisions or opinions that these Home Rule Cities find objectionable? Are you or your clients going to tell this court that although we are housed here in the City and County of Denver, that we have no jurisdiction in your state?"

"No, not that I am aware of, Your Honor. My colleagues made it abundantly clear that this court has jurisdiction under Title 28, United States Code, As Amended, Sections 1331 and 1343," she replied, stumbling over her words slightly.

"Then there is no difference between the Colorado State Supreme Court, and the United States Supreme Court has upheld jurisdiction within its own state borders, having jurisdiction over those same Home Rule Cities. Yes, I am aware that sometimes a court of law may make decisions, from time to time, that are unfavorable to some people. This Senate bill is no excuse for weakening the court that makes the unfavorable decision or opinion."

She turned to consult with her clients quickly before turning around and facing the judge once again. This time she was starting to get a flushed look on her face.

"Yes, Your Honor, my clients and I are aware, and do concede that sometimes a court of law makes unfavorable decisions to some people."

"All right, let's move on to Senate Bill SB19-2701, stating The Colorado State Supreme Court cannot invalidate voter referendums. Have you or your clients ever considered that voters may make mistakes passing laws that are contrary to either the state or the federal constitutions?"

"Your Honor, the purpose and intent of that Senate bill was to protect the Bill of Rights, specifically the 9th Amendment right of the voters as a whole, to pass laws that they see fit or think that they need."

"Okay, then, please tell this court what state prurient interest is at hand, here?"

She conferred with the clients for a short time before answering.

"The Senate bill, as stated earlier, is to protect the 9th Amendment right of the voters as a whole and to prevent the Colorado State Supreme Court from invalidating that right of the voters. The other smaller purpose was to prevent the Colorado State Supreme Court from violating the checks and balances system of a three-part system of government."

The timer started ringing and Ulysses shut it off.

"This court isn't entirely convinced of that statement, but, since we are out of time, it will have to do."

"Your Honor, my clients and I demand to know the real reason why we are here for this bogus emergency injunction," snapped Jodi.

"Plaintiffs?" asked Ulysses nicely, but he could tell trouble was brewing, and with a curt nod of his head and a quick left eye movement, the court Bailiff reached down and pushed the panic button three times. The Bailiff then moved towards the defendants with her right hand on her handcuff carrier case, unsnapping the carrier. She then gripped the handcuffs for immediate use in the courtroom.

"Your Honor, the CSSC is going to be forced, on the 14th of May of 2021, to violate the rights of the appealers without the injunction being granted even if only temporarily prior to a more formal hearing," said Della as she stood up, feeling the tension in the courtroom. Just outside the courtroom, three armed U.S. Marshals were waiting to burst into the courtroom if needed.

"Do you happen to know the particular case number?" asked Ulysses as he prepared to write it down.

"The case number is 20AP7719," replied Della calmly as Debbie Jo jumped out of her chair and flew into an uncontrolled rage, yelling at Della.

"You faggot loving bitch!"

Her attorney tried to calm her down as Ulysses started banging down his gavel.

"Order!, Order! Order in my courtroom! Ms. Torkelsen, if you cannot control your client, I will find her in contempt of my court!" he yelled, still banging down his gavel as her attorney wiped her face in total disbelief. The armed U.S. Marshals burst into the courtroom.

"You're a faggot lover, too, Dave Morgan! I'll see to it that you're disbarred along with anyone else who wants to protect them!" she yelled, trying to get at Della and Dave.

"You're in contempt of my court! Bailiff, remove her from my courtroom!" yelled Ulysses, banging down his gavel several more times.

The Bailiff moved in right away and put the handcuffs on Debbie Jo as the U.S. Marshals assisted with removing her. Judge Sorensen looked down at Jodi and Shelly with some disdain.

"Ms. Mortam or Mr. Morgan, now that you're not in any danger, do you know what she was talking about?"

Cautiously, they stood up, expecting Shelly to do the same thing. Dave kept an eye on her, which allowed Della to answer the question.

"Yes, Your Honor, we know what she was talking about," said Della rather demurely.

"Ms. Mortam, I want you to know that you have nothing to fear for telling this court the truth, no matter how painful the truth may be to some people. The job of a court of law is to get to the truth of a matter."

"Thank you, Your Honor. Appeals case number 20AP7719 is a combined appeals case testing the CSSC on whether or not it will overturn the convictions. Currently, the CSSC's hands are tied at the moment, along with the attorney who is representing and defending them along with the estimated 605,000 others living in the State of Colorado who are similarly situated."

"Thank you, Ms. Mortam and do you who know their attorney is?"

"Daniel Marcos, Your Honor."

The judge smiled when heard the name as he had heard it many times before from the other judges. He knew that Daniel was a very good attorney by their high praise of him.

"Please pass along to Mr. Marcos that this court says congratulations on being nominated as a possible replacement for the retiring Chief Justice John Wisenrock of the CSSC."

"I will certainly pass that along, Your Honor. The appeals case will challenge Colorado Revised Statutes, Title 18, Article 6, Part 800.3, Domestic Violence and the constitutionality of Article II, Section 31 of the Colorado State Constitution. Without an emergency injunction against the enforcement, in whole or in part, of those Senate bills, their appeals case cannot receive a fair hearing and the CSSC cannot rule properly or legally."

The judge sat quietly on his bench for a few minutes thinking heavily on what Della had just said. He had read between the lines of her statement to get the truth.

"In other words, Mr. Marcos' clients and those that you represent have same-sex marriages, civil unions, domestic partnerships or whatever other legal definition there is out there, don't they?"

"Yes, Your Honor."

"Do the defendants have anything else to add to this discussion?"

"No, Your Honor except that I wish to apologize for my client's inexcusable behavior in your courtroom."

"Apology accepted, Ms. Torkelsen. This case is hereby concluded and I will render my verdict on or about the 9th of April of 2021," he said, banging down his gavel, closing the case file and standing up to exit the courtroom.

"All rise," said the Bailiff.

Daniel turned off his computer and took the signed forms into Shilah's office. Shilah was in court in Durango again all day, so Daniel went home after arming the alarm system.

CHAPTER 8

The Speaker of the House and the Speaker of the Senate for the Colorado State legislature were looking at each other from across a table in the basement of the State Capitol building in Denver. The door was shut so that they had some privacy. The Speaker of the Senate had received the envelope a few weeks earlier. There was enough evidence in the envelope against four state Representatives and eight state Senators to begin the impeachment process on ethics violations.

"I thought that the Stockwell debacle in 2014 would have taught these people that they are not invincible. I mean, that information shows hate and animosity towards certain constituents; that's unethical," said the Speaker of the House, Morgan Gantry.

"So it would appear and these ethics violations go back for more than a decade," replied the Speaker of the Senate, Hannah Belle.

"You do know who would conduct the impeachment trials, right?" asked Morgan.

"It would be the sad duty of whoever replaces the retiring chief justice and I, personally, don't like any of the possible replacements with the exception of Daniel Marcos," said Hannah.

"If it isn't him, then would Associate Justice Tartik take the position?"

"Yes, and then the Good Ole' Boys club is back in action again. She would find her 'friends' on that list not guilty despite all of this evidence."

"I must say that I have to agree with you on that point, Hannah. Does Daniel Marcos have the qualifications to be the chief justice?"

"He's a former public defender, a former prosecutor and current criminal defense attorney. He allegedly specializes in high profile and/or high risk clients."

There came a knock on the door; Hannah motioned for silence and opened the door. The waiter was there with their lunch orders. Hannah tipped him and then closed the door again. As they ate lunch, the talk turned back to Daniel; Morgan wiped her mouth.

"Does Daniel have his Jurist Doctorate degree, and does he meet the other constitutional requirements for the position?"

"I know he meets the minimum age and residency requirements. I'm not sure about the others; I'll try and find out. Do you know what political party he is affiliated with?"

"No, perhaps the Constitutional Party or maybe he's an Independent."

"I'll check with the Elections Commission on that one, but he needs about 600,000 voter signatures to get on the ballot, right?"

"Oh, I think his group of volunteers could get that done easily enough. You know, if he's elected, he would be considered a dark horse and we know all too well what happens to dark horses."

"Unfortunately, yes."

They finished off their lunch and Hannah handed Morgan a piece of paper with recommended instructions for her speech to the state house delegates; they both departed after shaking hands. They returned to their respective chambers to deliver their welcome speeches. In the House of Representatives, when the welcome speech was almost over, Morgan delivered the final paragraph to the delegates.

"As you are well aware, we all took an oath, today, to represent not only ourselves and our respective house districts, but all the constituents in those respective districts."

Morgan paused before continuing.

"Let me remind everyone here that Article IV, Section IV of the U.S. Constitution guarantees that all of the states shall have a republic form of government. This republic form of government is made up of those chosen by their constituency to represent them and to govern them. Some of you in this chamber are heading down the same road as your colleagues did in 2014 with the Stockwell impeachment trials."

She paused again and looked right into the eyes of the four from the list. The sergeant at arms looked over at her with his mouth wide open in astonishment.

"Let me make this unmistakably clear to all of you. If you hate and show animosity towards your constituency, either because of religious or personal reasons, you need not be a Representative any longer. If you cannot treat your entire constituency with respect and dignity, you're in violation of the ethics part of the oath we just took. Make no mistake about it; four of you in this chamber are facing possible impeachment proceedings. That is not an idle threat; that is a promise; thank you."

She turned to face the Sergeant-At-Arms.

"We will take a ten minute break and then reconvene for business for the 127th General Assembly," she said, banging down her gavel. A similar speech was being given in the Senate.

"Make no mistake about it; eight of you in these chambers are headed down the same road as your colleagues did in 2014 with the Stockwell impeachment trials. Let me make this clear, the Good Ole' Boys club is over and done with. If you cannot properly or ethically treat your constituency fairly and with dignity because of personal or religious prejudices, and if you feel that the only way you can justify being an elected Senator of your respective Senate districts is to discriminate against your constituency or show racist views towards them, then you need not be an elected Senator any more. I will gladly accept your resignation or your letter of intent not to run for reelection."

She paused before going on.

"If you think for one minute that the Good Ole' Boys club will protect you, you're sadly mistaken. The threat of impeachment on the basis of violating the ethics part of the oath is no empty threat, it's a promise. Hate and animosity directed at your constituency is unacceptable even if to you it is an acceptable family value."

She paused once more before finishing off her welcome speech.

"You were sent here to represent your constituency, and you would be wise to remember that before pouring forth hate and animosity towards them; thank you," she said, banging down her gavel.

When the session had been completed for the day, the Sergeant-At-Arms entered Hannah's office. He knocked on her inner office door before entering.

"Madam Speaker, I'm getting ready to lock up the chambers for the weekend; is there anything else I can do for you?" he asked.

"Yes, I want you to do something for me during this session. I am asking you to do this because, if I do it, someone will get suspicious."

He raised his left eyebrow a little and took out his black notebook and pen.

"Go ahead, Madam Speaker."

"You do understand that you are considered, by Colorado Revised Statutes Criminal Code, Title 18, as being a person in a position of trust; right?"

"Yes, I understand and know that I may be found guilty of violating Title 18 of Colorado Revised Statutes under a lot of different circumstances."

"Good; Morgan and I feel that there's a high probability that the current chief justice of the state Supreme Court may not make it to the end of the current court session. Therefore, I need you to find me fifteen volunteer Senators who are willing to stay after the close of the regular session to do an emergency confirmation hearing if needed and as provided for under the Senate bylaws."

She paused while he wrote things down. When the pen had stopped moving she spoke again.

"There is also a general feeling that Daniel Marcos will be the one picked personally by retiring Chief Justice John Wisenrock to replace him. Neither I, Morgan, nor our other colleagues have anything personally against the other candidates; they all have political ambitions. This makes them less suited for the job of interpreting and applying the constitution and the laws that the legislature passes."

"I have heard some of the Senators refer to Daniel Marcos as a dark horse."

"Yes, he is a dark horse, and that's where you come in for the other favor. Do you have any contacts over at the Colorado Bar?"

"Yes, I was at Dianne's wedding as the best man, I guess that is what you would call it."

"Good, I want you to see if Daniel Marcos has, in his Bar file, under tab four, his Jurist Doctorate degree and his other credentials for being a judge. I'm sure that Dianne can assist with that issue. I also want you to prepare the Senate chamber for possible impeachment trials."

"I've already done that, Madam Speaker; I picked up on your speech you gave today."

"You're very astute, Sergeant-At-Arms. I trust that what we discussed here is confidential?"

"Absolutely, Madam Speaker, and I know that my opinion doesn't count for much, but I signed the petition to put Daniel's name on the November ballot."

"I did the same thing; dismissed."

When Daniel arrived home one night from a late court appearance in Durango, Chayton asked him something at the dinner table he wasn't really prepared for.

"Dad, what's a dark arse?"

"Well, the word arse is German for butt. So it means dark butt."

"Oh, then why do Cindy's mom and Dad think you have a dark butt, Dad?"

Todd was starting to laugh at this time at this little exchange.

"I don't know."

After a couple more bites of mashed potatoes, Daniel figured out what Cindy's mom and Dad had been talking about.

"Chayton, I think the term that Cindy's mom and Dad were using was dark horse."

"I don't think you're a dark horse either, Dad."

"The term dark horse doesn't refer to an animal. It is a political term used for someone who the political types and the general public know almost nothing about."

"Oh, I see; thanks Dad."

On one of his weekend trips to Denver to visit his all-volunteer campaign headquarters, he ran into a middle aged man who was heckling him. The man was yelling all sorts of things at him from polygamy to legalizing drugs. When he was through with yelling his taunts, Daniel turned to face him and his support crew of protesters. After Daniel signed a few more autographs and some more pictures were taken of him, he smiled as a member of his staff ran up to the man with a pen and a pad of paper to take notes. When she was close enough, the man spit in her face. She wiped it off with a handkerchief as he spoke harshly to her.

"Faggot lover!" he said, not aware of the presence of a cell phone camera, just inches away, that had recorded the whole incident.

The crowd of Daniel Marcos supporters was about to lynch the man, when Daniel raised his hands to stop the advancing crowd.

"Don't give in to him, because that is what he wants. Let me forewarn you, sir, that if the young lady there wants to press charges against you, she can. The charge would be Third Degree Assault," said Daniel, before continuing.

"Now, to answer your first question, legalizing prostitution is a very complicated undertaking. My clients are very keenly aware of that daunting task; my clients further wish to have no part of that."

"Prostitution is legal in Nevada; why not here?" he yelled.

"Although the State of Nevada legalized prostitution many decades ago and it produces some very handsome tax revenue, it is still illegal in five counties."

"It's legal in Las Vegas!" he shouted, as the crowd of supporters behind him shouted at Daniel.

"Prostitution is not legal in Las Vegas, and that is where the mainstream media has lied to us all over the past few decades. Prostitution is illegal in the county where the City of Las Vegas is located. If you think that I am lying to you, please give that nice young lady there your contact information, and I will mail the answer to you so that you can have it for future reference."

"Okay, you may have gotten me on that issue, but what about polygamy and bigamy. I mean, isn't that what the Mormon religion teaches?"

"Again, that's where the mainstream media has lied to us. The Mormons were never polygamists or bigamists. The Founders of that religion, Joseph Smith and Brigham Young, never advocated for marrying more than one woman. This was done to protect the role that traditional marriage would play in our country."

He paused before continuing.

"To answer the second part of your question, polygamy/bigamy has been and always will be illegal in all states that joined the Union at the end of the Civil War and after the ratification of the 14th Amendment to the U.S. Constitution. It was also illegal in those states that joined the Union prior to the war. There is a really nice op-ed piece in the *Daily Sentinel* out of Grand Junction if you're interested in reading more about it."

The man was almost as stunned by this revelation as were some of the protesters; he didn't let it stop him.

"What about bestiality and pedophilia? Aren't your clients for that type of stuff?"

"Generally speaking, my clients and those similarly situated, are for stronger penalties and more enforcement of the current laws on the books in all fifty states and civilized countries throughout the world. Because you asked, most pedophiles are, sadly enough, heterosexual or straight. For more information, please refer to the Belfour Study at www.belfourstudy.org."

"You and your clients are Pro-Choice!"

"Generally speaking, my clients are Pro-Lifers."

"And you?"

"Pro-Life."

"What about your clients wanting to legalize all drugs?"

"It cannot be done because it is way too complicated now. Again, if you will kindly give your contact information to that young lady there, I will respond in writing to your inquiry in a week or so."

"Do you have any political ambitions?"

"No, all I want is for truth and justice to prevail on the bench. I also want that to apply to any case that comes before the bench."

"Your clients want to be able to marry their brother or sister; what do you have to say about that?"

"Again, the mainstream media has lied to us. My clients, generally speaking, are for stronger penalties and more enforcement of the laws that are currently on the books that prohibit such behavior."

"You and your clients are going to force the churches to recognize same-sex marriages and civil unions."

"Again, the mainstream media has lied to us all. No church or other religious organization has ever been forced by the state to recognize, abide by or validate a same-sex marriage or civil union in those states where such things are legal."

The man stopped short of asking his next questions and decided to give his contact information to the lady. She then walked back to where Daniel was standing.

"I was about to punch his lights out, Mr. Marcos," she said.

"I understand, and I'm glad you didn't do it. I'm very proud and honored to have someone like you on my all-volunteer staff. If you had punched his lights out, you would have been no better than him. He would have succeeded in dragging you down to his level of ignorance. Besides, the crowd was getting a little restless and, had you hit him, I can almost guarantee that a riot would have broken out."

"I have his contact information."

"Good, when we all get back to the campaign headquarters, I'll write up a nice letter and send him copies of everything I told him about today."

"Mr. Marcos, I can hardly write a letter home to my family, let alone write a nice letter to someone who just spit in my face on TV."

"I understand; is there someone else who can help me with that person's issues?"

"He can," she said pointing to a handsome, red-headed boy with long sideburns and a goatee. Daniel guessed that he was in his early twenties.

Everyone walked back to the campaign headquarters and went to work. The kid showed Daniel no less than five prototype letters. Daniel looked them over, crossed out what he didn't like about them and handed them back. After an hour and half, the kid returned with the finished product. Daniel looked it over and signed the letter at the bottom. He then put this into the small box of paperwork going to the heckler first thing Monday morning.

The kid soon returned from the post office and showed Daniel the latest attack ads from his competitors. When the last attack ad had played, Daniel sat back in his chair to think.

"Mr. Marcos, you need to respond to those attack ads," said the kid.

"No, and I'm going to tell you why. Unlike my esteemed colleagues, there will be no mudslinging in this campaign from my camp. To do so would bring us down to their level. Is that clear to this campaign staff?"

They all nodded their heads.

"We've put together some testimonials for the campaign," said one of the women.

"Fine, let me look them over and, if I approve, run them. By the way, how much money does my campaign fund have?"

"More than $11,000,000.00," said the kid with the red hair.

"I see and who is bank rolling this campaign?"

"My Dad and I," he replied.

"I hope you two understand that I will not be able to get elected."

"You will; the campaign is working to do just that. Are you going to debate your colleagues?" he asked.

"No."

Daniel paused a minute or two before finishing his thought.

"A hundred years ago, I would have debated my colleagues, as you call them, because the debate would have been about laws and legal issues. Today, my colleagues would use the debate forum for pitching unsubstantiated accusations at me and other things not related to law. Prepare some material for my own ads and email them to me. If you'll excuse me, I have to catch the last flight home," said Daniel as he left campaign headquarters for DIA.

CHAPTER 9

April 9th, 2021 had arrived. Della and Dave were in the courtroom along with Jodi and her clients. All were eagerly awaiting the judge's decision on the injunction request. It was 2:45 p.m. when the Bailiff stood up; so did the rest of the court. Daniel had logged into the website to see what the verdict was going to be.

"All rise; the 10th Federal Circuit Court is now in session. The Honorable Chief Judge Ulysses Lyle Sorensen, presiding, over the case of *The State of Colorado V. Della Mortam and Dave Morgan Et. Al.*, case number 21CV0116-ULS."

The judge walked up the stairs to his bench and sat down.

"You may be seated and this court will come to order. These proceedings are being recorded and broadcast on www.federalcourtstv.gov/10thFederalCircuit/ULS/21CV0116-ULS.htm, or on TV Channels 501 and 503. These are in accordance with the directives from the 9th Federal Circuit Court following the Proposition 8 trial."

He paused before continuing.

"Are the plaintiffs in this case present in the courtroom?"

Dave and Della stood up nervously.

"We are, Your Honor," said Della.

"Please remain standing and thank you. Are the defendants in this case present?"

Jodi stood with her clients as did the two U.S. Marshals standing near Senator Debbie Jo Donovan, or D.J. as she was sometimes called by her constituents, in case she got out of hand again.

"We are, Your Honor," said Jodi.

"Very well, please remain standing. Let me remind you, Senator Donovan, if you get out of hand again in my courtroom you will have to deal with me, the stun gun and the handcuffs. Do I make myself clear, Madam?"

"Crystal clear, Your Honor, all I want to do is go back to working for my constituency."

There was another pause while he shuffled papers around on his bench.

"The official and full opinion of this court will be released, in accordance with current court rules as amended, in ten business days. This court, after carefully reviewing and weighing the arguments presented from both sides of this case, finds for the plaintiffs. The Senate bills so named in the opinion are unconstitutional under the 14th Amendment. This court also finds evidence that the Senate bills so named also violate the checks and balances system that is in place in all state constitutions as well as the federal constitution."

He paused.

"The finding is not only for the plaintiffs, but also extends to those in this case that are similarly situated. Do either the plaintiffs or the defendants wish to appeal this court's decision on the granting of the emergency injunction and declaratory relief?" asked Ulysses.

"No, Your Honor, we do not wish to appeal," said Dave quickly.

"So noted."

Ms. Torkelsen conferred with her clients for a short time before turning back around to face the judge.

"We wish to appeal," she said.

"So noted; a three judge panel will review this case on or about the 3rd of November, 2021."

"Thank you, Your Honor."

"This case is on appeal, but the injunction will be enforced until a further ruling is handed down. Mr. Morgan and Ms. Mortam, please tell the chief justice of the Colorado State Supreme Court that this court wishes him and the associate justices good luck on the appeals case that they are facing; next case, Bailiff."

Dave and Della rushed out of the courtroom and out of the courthouse. Daniel was shocked and very relieved at the same time by the judge's ruling. He made sure to notate on his electronic calendar when the tenth business day would be, so he could download the entire court opinion for later reading.

Daniel was preparing his opening statements to the Colorado State Supreme Court in just a few short weeks. He decided that when this case was finally over, whenever that was going to be, he would go to the museum to become one of their newest directors. He was packing up some last minute items to take to the storage area in the mountain when the phone rang.

"Hello?" asked Daniel.

"Good afternoon, Skipper, this is your friendly XO, here; just wanted to let you know that the enemy fleet has suffered a serious setback. However, they did launch a cruise missile attack."

"So, should I take evasive action?"

"No, you're well out of cruise missile range."

"Great; who is this?"

"Daniel, I thought you knew who your XO was; it's Leslie."

"The same Leslie who was once an associate justice of the state supreme court?"

"Yes."

"I thought the voice sounded familiar. What about my disbarment for speaking out on same-sex marriages?"

"There's been a disarming of that bomb for you by Chief Judge Ulysses Lyle Sorensen of the 10th Federal Circuit Court."

"But, I'm still carrying a very large nuclear weapon so to speak."

"Yes and you're carrying it in a rickety old plane, shot full of holes and flying with only one, very badly smoking engine. The Group is most impressed with the fact that you and your crew have kept it flying despite the anti-aircraft fire that the enemy has put up to try and stop you."

"Why, thank you, XO, but I will still have to be prepared for the possible contingency plan that I will be disbarred."

"Don't be so quick to judge someone, Daniel. Because of your stances on certain key issues and because I don't think many people like the possible replacements, you're it. By the way, have you read the morning paper yet?"

"No."

"Rick Sanchez quit his job under the threat of being indicted under ethics violations by the American Bar Association."

"Who replaced him?"

"For the time being, The Group has decided that Dianne Tolmage will be in charge until someone more suitable applies and is hired."

"She's a good person; I've met her a few times."

"The Group seems to think so as well, Daniel, but she doesn't see herself in that light."

"By the way, who is this alleged Group?"

"We will reveal ourselves to you in time. For right now, don't give up the fight for your clients or those similarly situated. In other words, drop that nuclear weapon on them. Those people fear you down there in the religious stronghold of both the United States and Colorado."

"I will do my best at the project I have undertaken. Do they know that I've figured out the one weakness in their laws?"

"Yes, and they know you're going to exploit it. You may not know this, but you have some very powerful friends on the state supreme court."

"I believe former Appellate Court Judge Donna Pinewood said something like that to me a few months ago."

"She's a good woman and a good judge of character."

"You know that dark horse candidates like me usually have short careers."

"Sometimes; sometimes it becomes necessary to clean house, so to speak."

"I can't argue with you on that issue."

"Goodbye, Daniel, and on behalf of myself and The Group, we wish you good luck."

"Thank you, I'm going to need it; goodbye," said Daniel, hanging up the phone.

Daniel, Todd and Chayton all packed up their clothes and other things they were going to need for the one day trip they all hoped they were going on. Daniel locked up the house, drove to the Durango airport and they all boarded an old 737-900C series jet. As the landing gear thumped aboard the plane, another set of landing gear was coming down with the same thump.

The Boeing 767-400ER chartered aircraft was on final approach to DIA. Seth looked over at Tyler and then down at their twin boys. Seth gripped Tyler's right hand very tightly as the plane was touching down. As the pilot guided the plane onto the taxiway, Seth spoke to Tyler.

"Is it too late to turn back?"

"No, we have plenty of fuel to get us back to the refueling point; do you really want to turn around?"

"No."

The plane taxied to the far end of the tarmac, pulling into one of the private hangars for commercial jets. When the door had opened and the engines were shutdown, a Customs Agent came aboard for an inspection. Seth, Tyler and their boys cleared customs. Seth obtained a rental car and they all drove to the same hotel where Daniel was staying.

As Daniel's plane was pulling up to Gate B-34, Daniel rented a car as well, driving them all to the hotel. Daniel, Todd and Chayton walked into the hotel lobby which was filled with reporters. Daniel politely pushed past them all, saying, "No comment." Once they had finally checked in, Daniel, Todd and Chayton went up the 17th floor to their suite. As Daniel was trying to shut the door, a reporter stopped the door with his left hand.

"Mr. Marcos, you have a lot of supporters out there in Civic Center Park," he said, earnestly hoping Daniel would buy it because it was the truth.

"Really? How many protestors are out there as well?"

"I haven't really counted the exact number, but I estimate that they number at least 10,000."

"And how many of my supporters, as you call them, do I allegedly have?"

"I haven't really counted the exact number there, either, but I estimate they number at least 75,000. The word got out on various social networking sites about you fighting for the legalization of same-sex marriages in Colorado."

He paused before continuing.

"You will have a human shield with which to walk to and from the Supreme Court building as many times as you need to."

"I see; tell my supporters thank you and are you aware of the fact that if I bring up the issue of legalizing same-sex marriages, I will be disbarred?"

"I have heard the rumors about that being a major hurdle to get over."

"Well, it is a fact, not a rumor, and you now have something to think about; goodnight, sir," said Daniel, as he finally was able to get the door shut.

United Airlines flight 779 from Nashville, Tennessee, was landing at DIA with a very important passenger aboard; District Court Judge Lynn Lyons-Seagate. She deplaned, secured a rental car and then retrieved her luggage. Suddenly a right hand grabbed her left hand. Lynn looked up the arm to see Jessica Kim, her husband and their kids.

"Mind if we tag along?" asked Jessica.

"Absolutely, where do you want me to take you?" Lynn asked as she started to cry with tears of joy.

"Sure, how about downtown to the Marriot®?"

"Let's go," said Lynn, as they all tossed their luggage into the back of Lynn's rental car and drove off.

Delta Airlines redeye flight 1615 from Atlanta, Georgia, was landing at DIA with a very important passenger aboard; Dr. Bill Lazlo. He deplaned, obtained a taxi to take him and his luggage to the downtown Holiday Inn®. He checked into the hotel and fell asleep almost immediately.

The next morning was the final round of chemotherapy and radiation treatments for Chief Justice Wisenrock. He was sitting in the comfortable chair next to the machine that was pumping him full of chemicals to fight his particular form of cancer. The doctor returned to the room, removed the empty bag and needles from Chief Justice Wisenrock's right arm. Chief Justice Wisenrock was now looking emaciated from all of the treatments. The doctor then checked Chief Justice Wisenrock's vital signs and let him go.

Chief Justice Wisenrock went home and took a three hour nap before heading into court. Before court began, the Bailiff would strategically place several trashcans around the chief justice's chair for him to throw up into. As court was convening for the day, Daniel, Todd and Chayton were downstairs in the hotel's lobby trying to have breakfast while being constantly interrupted by reporters who wanted to ask questions or take pictures or both.

Daniel noticed that News Channel 7 was turned on and then he saw the headline: "IS THE SAME-SEX MARRIAGE DEBATE HEADED TO THE COLORADO STATE SUPREME COURT?" Daniel then saw all the protestors in the background waving their hate filled signs. He then saw the supporters filling up the streets surrounding Civic Center Park in front of the Capitol Building.

"The hate flows heavily today," said Daniel as he finished his breakfast.

They all went back up to their hotel room; Daniel left Todd in charge of Chayton. He told Todd what channel to watch in the hotel room so that Chayton could see and hear his dad. Daniel also left instructions not to answer the telephone or answer the door for anyone. When Daniel closed the door, Todd threw the deadbolt into place along with the door latch located about half way up the door. He turned on the hotel room's TV to channel 515. Daniel exited the hotel right into the human shield of his supporters. One of the supporters, a seven foot tall, 300 pound man stood out.

"Mr. Marcos, we all wish you the best of luck, and we can guarantee safe passage to the front steps of the Supreme Court building and back."

"Thank you."

"Just follow the tunnel of people."

Daniel walked through the gauntlet of people to the steps of the Supreme Court building. He walked up the steps and looked up at the words on the building's entrance; "**LIBERTY AND JUSTICE FOR ALL**." Daniel bowed his head down and went about putting his briefcase on the X-ray machine belt to continue through security. Security was unusually tight as Daniel went through both the metal detector and then he was patted down by one of the courthouse security officers. Having cleared through security, he picked up his briefcase off of the X-ray machine belt and headed down the hallway towards the Supreme Court's chambers. He approached a set of wooden double-doors on which hung a familiar sign; "QUIET COURT IS IN SESSION."

Soon, Daniel's clients arrived. He took them down the hallway to an attorney/client room that was unoccupied and unlocked. They all filed into the little room with their kids and sat down.

"Do you want me to quit, or do you want me to go all the way? I'm only asking this because my esteemed colleague, Mr. Fargo, is going to ask me that question," said Daniel.

"We go all the way to the U.S. Supreme Court, if necessary," they all said in sequence.

"Okay, everyone, just remain calm for now. We have about an hour and a half before our case comes up," said Daniel, looking up at the clock on the wall.

Seth, Tyler and the twins had just cleared security. Tyler took the twins downstairs to the daycare center that was located in the basement and returned. Seth was talking to Lynn and Marshal Halverston, the Ironton Town Marshal. Standing next to Marshal Halverston was Marshal Gills, the Silverton Town Marshal.

"Have you seen him yet, Seth?" asked Tyler.

"No, do you think he's still at the hotel?" replied Seth.

"I don't think so; remember, we knocked on his door and there was no answer," said Tyler.

The crowd started to become larger as the time closed in on Daniel and his clients. A short recess was called by Chief Justice Wisenrock before Daniel's case came up. Daniel saw the time and decided that it would be a good idea to get a seat in the courtroom during the break. When Daniel opened the left side door of the double wooden doors, he walked into a room filled with familiar faces. As Daniel, his clients and their kids filed into the courtroom, Mr. Fargo bumped into Daniel.

"I have your disbarment paperwork ready to go when you bring up legalizing same-sex marriages," Mr. Fargo gloated.

"We shall see, Mr. Fargo," said Daniel as he sat down in his chair at the table labeled "PLAINTIFFS." Brian grabbed Daniel's right arm.

"You look really nice today, Daniel. Win or lose, you, your family, and your friends, come to my restaurant to eat dinner."

"You're on, and thank you."

Mr. Fargo touched Daniel on Daniel's left arm.

"There's still time to bail out."

"No dice, Mr. Fargo."

"Better watch out, it looks like Brian, there, wants to cheat on his husband with you," sneered Mr. Fargo.

"Maybe, but a more logical explanation would be Proverbs 27 verse 21. No, Mr. Fargo, my clients and I are going all the way."

Daniel watched as Mr. Fargo had to look up the particular passage on his PDA.

CHAPTER 10

Daniel did a quick scan of the spectator's box behind him and found a lot more familiar faces. A lot of people had filed into the spectator's box. Daniel now realized how important this appeals case really was. Soon, the entire courtroom was packed with people including the press box to Daniel's left in the balcony area.

There were the talk radio stations KHOW AM630, Progressive Talk Radio AM760 and News Talk Radio KOA AM850; Denver News Channels 4, 7 and 9 were present as well. When Daniel looked behind him at the press box, there were Representatives from CNN News®, Fox31 News, and La Gratia Channel 47, serving the Latino community. Daniel then looked to his right and saw that this press box was filled with Representatives from the BBC, PBS, NPR and Court TV.com. They stood up when the Bailiff stood.

"All rise, the Colorado State Supreme Court is now in session. The Honorable Chief Justice John Wisenrock, presiding, over the case of *Patricia Duffy-Downs et. al. v. The State of Colorado*; case number 20AP7719."

As the justices filed into the courtroom, Daniel was able to get a good look at them. Associate Justice Caroline Hayes looked right at Daniel and mouthed the words "bastard" at him. Associate Justice Hayes was average in height and weight with blue eyes, short black hair, which showed some gray in it. She wore wire framed glasses through which she glared at Daniel. She was one of the oldest women on the Supreme Court bench at sixty-six.

Next in line, to Associate Justice Hayes' right, was Associate Justice Darcy Smith. She was short in stature and her chair at the bench had to have two Denver telephone books placed on it in order for her to see above the microphone. She was a Latina, and kept her auburn hair pulled back into a bun. She wore contact lenses so that she didn't have to carry around the bulky eyeglass case. She was second in age to Justice Hayes on the bench at sixty.

Next in line, to Associate Justice Smith's right, was Associate Justice Carson Robins. He was of African-American heritage with chiseled facial features. He wore thick framed, brown colored eye glasses that were attached to a small chain. He was stoic, looking out across the spectator's box and then down at Mr. Fargo. Justice Robins was 6 feet 7 inches tall and weighed in at over 300 pounds with a shiny, bald head. To Daniel, Associate Justice Robins was an African-American version of Orson Wells. He was also the oldest Supreme Court justice on the bench at seventy-nine.

Next in line, to Associate Justice Robins' right, was Chief Justice Wisenrock. He was smaller, now, than Daniel had remembered him being the last time he had seen him. His face was an ashen white color and his eyes were sunk slightly back into his skull. He was also very weak and had no hair left on his head. Chief Justice Wisenrock was only sixty-one years old, but Daniel began to feel that this would be his last case in this courtroom. The cancer and the treatments for it had taken their toll on him.

Next in line, to Chief Justice Wisenrock's right, was Associate Justice Regina Tartik. She was glaring at Daniel and his clients as well as the spectator's box. She wore contact lenses as well, stood almost 6 feet in height and had red hair; she was also of thin build. She was the youngest of the women Supreme Court justices at forty-nine. Daniel looked at her right hand to see her flipping Daniel off.

Standing next in line, to her right, was Associate Justice Vince Kathryn. Vince was the second youngest Supreme Court justice at age fifty-five. He was still sporting a full head of blond hair and was somewhat heavyset; he smiled at Daniel and his clients.

Finally, the newest member of the Supreme Court bench was Associate Justice Bianca Hale. She was only fifty years old with flowing, long black hair. She was of average height and weight. She wore no glasses or contact lenses and stood tall and proud at the bench while the news reporters snapped pictures and shot video for the evening news. Soon, they all sat down.

"You may be seated and this court will come to order," said Chief Justice Wisenrock in almost a whisper while banging down his gavel.

"These proceedings are being recorded and broadcast at both www.coloradocourtstv.gov\CSSC\20AP7719.htm as well as on TV channels 505, 515, 525 and 530. All of this is in accordance with the directives of the 9th Federal Circuit Court from the Proposition 8 trial. This court would like to recognize Attorney Daniel Marcos as being a possible and much preferred replacement for me on this bench," he said as the whole room broke out into clapping. Chief Justice Wisenrock suddenly reached for one of the trashcans and threw up into it; wiping his mouth off with a tissue.

"Over my dead body, Your Honor," muttered Associate Justice Hayes, hoping Chief Justice Wisenrock would hear what she had said.

"I'm sorry you feel that away, Associate Justice Hayes," said Chief Justice Wisenrock, hoarsely once again. He paused before continuing.

"Periodically, Ladies and Gentlemen of the court, due to my illness, I will be throwing up in trashcans near my seat here on the bench. If this offends anyone, you may leave now. This is an appeals case brought forth to the court of last resort via the Appellate Court system, upon a request of the plaintiffs having invoked Rule 113, Section D of the Appellate Court Code. Are the plaintiffs in this case present in this courtroom?" asked Chief Justice Wisenrock as he put on his reading glasses. Daniel stood up.

"We are, Your Honor," replied Daniel as he sat back down.

"So noted; are the defendants represented, or in this case, the State represented, in this courtroom?"

"Yes, Your Honor, the State is represented in the courtroom."

"So noted," said Chief Justice Wisenrock as he bent down to his left and away from the microphone to throw up again into a trashcan. Once again, he wiped his mouth with a tissue.

"Are both parties prepared with opening statements?" asked Chief Justice Wisenrock.

"We are, Your Honor," said Daniel standing up and then sitting back down.

"We are, Your Honor," said Mr. Fargo standing up and then sitting back down.

"Very well, the State may present its opening statements to the court," said Chief Justice Wisenrock, as he leaned back into his chair.

"Thank you, Your Honor, and if it pleases the court, the State wants the convictions upheld as being legal despite what my esteemed colleague has to say about the matter. Mr. Marcos' clients broke the law and were found guilty of breaking the law by a jury of their peers. This was all done in accordance with the 6th Amendment to the federal constitution. The State sees nothing wrong with what they did; thank you," he said, sitting down.

"Very well, and thank you, Mr. Fargo, for being so brief for this court," said Chief Justice Wisenrock as he tried to swallow more bile that was ebbing up in the back of his throat.

"You're welcome, Your Honor," said Mr. Fargo, with confidence.

"The plaintiffs may begin their opening statements to the court," said Chief Justice Wisenrock.

Daniel stood up, shuffled his notes around and took in a deep breath to relax himself. He looked at all of the justices before finally speaking.

"Good morning, Your Honor, and if it pleases the court, my clients wish to have their convictions invalidated by this court due to an error in the law. This error in the law was further complicated by the same prosecutor who is currently running for the office of the State Attorney General."

He shuffled his notes around again and then went on with his opening statements.

"My clients were convicted of a crime, for which they cannot be convicted of, due to their second class citizenship, in this state. This lower class of citizenship was created by the voters of this state in 2006. This court knows this voter referendum as Article II, Section 31 of the Colorado State Constitution."

He looked up to see at least two of the justices taking notes on this case.

"The crime which my clients were convicted of requires a two-prong test to be passed before being considered a crime. The crime my clients were convicted of was Domestic Violence. The Domestic Violence statute in this state requires an intimate relationship AND a crime that was committed. My client's intimate relationship doesn't exist in the eyes of that law or of the law, period."

"Objection, Your Honor, the State clearly stated that Mr. Marcos' clients' intimate relationships meet the requirements of the *People V. Disher* case," said Ken.

Before Chief Justice Wisenrock could rule on the objection, Daniel pounced on the opportunity to start tearing down the State's evidence.

"I'm sorry, Your Honor, my client's intimate relationships and those similarly situated in this state, are nowhere near meeting the requirements of the Disher case," said Daniel.

"Would you not at least contend that your clients are exclusively dating, Mr. Marcos?" asked Associate Justice Tartik.

Chief Justice Wisenrock finally answered the objection.

"Objection is overruled."

"My clients are well beyond that requirement, Your Honor, and that case only involved a heterosexual couple, as the law was intended to prosecute."

"I see, but you stated in your court paperwork that there were numerous constitutional rights violations," said Associate Justice Hayes.

"That's right, Your Honor, my clients weren't going to lie on the witness stand while under oath, because that would be perjury. The prosecution violated their 5th Amendment constitutional protection against self-incrimination and the judge presiding over all three cases saw nothing wrong with it."

Justice Hayes looked down at Daniel sternly.

"How are your client's convictions an error of the law in which you specifically named Colorado's Defense of Marriage Act or DOMA?"

"Your Honor, my client's intimate relationships and those similarly situated in this state are not valid or recognized in this state. Without their intimate relationship being valid or recognized, the crime of Domestic Violence cannot exist."

Chief Justice Wisenrock, who had been slightly dozing off in his chair suddenly sat straight up and almost stood up.

"Good Lord, Mr. Marcos, do mean to tell this court that your clients have same-sex marriages?"

"Yes, Your Honor, they do. One from the State of Vermont, one from the State of New York and one from Toronto, Canada; I am aware, Your Honor, that the State of Colorado is one of five states that recognizes foreign marriages."

"You're correct, Mr. Marcos, but do you know who validated and recognized their marriages?" asked Justice Robins.

"The prosecutor did, Your Honor, by asking my clients, while they were on the witness stand, if they were married. Again, my clients didn't want to commit perjury, so they answered the question, as it was worded to them, truthfully."

The associate justices all looked at Chief Justice Wisenrock for some guidance.

"This court will have to take a short recess in order to get in touch with Mr. Killam and ask him about these cases," said Chief Justice Wisenrock, standing up and banging down his gavel. The justices all filed out the room.

"All rise," said the Bailiff.

After the justices had filed out of the courtroom and the front door to the courtroom was shut, Ken smiled, and handed Daniel his disbarment paperwork. Suddenly an arm came down from Daniel's left side and grabbed the paperwork.

"I'll take that from you, Mr. Fargo, and I, as a legal advisor to the American Bar Association, wish to inform you that Mr. Marcos is appealing this possible disbarment pending the results of a thorough investigation into the Colorado Bar Association's doings."

"And just who do you think you are?" he barked.

"1st Judicial District Court Judge Lynn Lyons-Seagate from the State of Tennessee," she replied, showing him her judicial ID.

"I see," said Ken, sitting quietly back down in his chair.

The Bailiff stood up, as did the rest of the courtroom, while the justices all filed into their respective positions on the bench.

"You married David Seagate?" asked Daniel, quietly, but in shock.

"Yes, I did, and being married to a billionaire has its advantages," she replied, winking at Daniel.

"All rise, the Colorado State Supreme Court is now in session. The Honorable Chief Justice John Wisenrock, presiding, over the case of *Patricia Duffy-Downs et. al. v. The State of Colorado*; case number 20AP7719."

"You may be seated, and this court will come to order. Before anyone says anything further, this court has called upon the current State Attorney General for clarification on this potentially legally sticky issue. Mr. Toole, can you hear me?" asked Chief Justice Wisenrock into the speaker of the telephone that was sitting on his desktop.

"I sure can, Your Honor, and it is a pleasure to be able to address the state supreme court this morning," said Sam.

"Thank you, Mr. Toole. In the context of criminal law, specifically the Domestic Violence statute, does that statute apply to same-sex couples in this state?" asked Chief Justice Wisenrock.

"Sadly enough, Your Honor, it appears that it doesn't. The Colorado voters, when they passed the Defense of Marriage Act, inadvertently created a protected class of citizens."

"And just why not?!" snapped Associate Justice Hayes, almost standing up at her position on the bench.

"A same-sex couple's intimate relationship is legally defined as a particularly close, interpersonal relationship involving physical or emotional intimacy. Physical intimacy is characterized by romantic or passionate love and attachment, or sexual activity. A same-sex couple is further protected, legally speaking, by the fact that the Defense of Marriage Act, or DOMA, recognizes only heterosexual unions, i.e., traditional marriages."

"If a prosecutor has recognized and validated a same-sex couple's intimate relationship, in this case, their same-sex marriages, do the convictions of Domestic Violence, under Colorado Law, apply?" asked Associate Justice Smith.

"I do not think so, Your Honor. If the prosecutor knew full well that they were same-sex couples when the cases were presented to him, then he should have either let the cases go or charged them with a lesser crime."

"I see; would you defend the Defense of Marriage Act in this court if it were challenged?" asked Associate Justice Kathryn.

"Absolutely not, Your Honor. I am not, nor can I defend something in good conscience, that is so racist, prejudiced and discriminatory within this state's constitution."

"Would you not consider that the clients did have intimate relationships to justify their convictions?" asked Associate Justice Hayes.

"No, the only way I might be able to see a conviction on the charge of Domestic Violence in this state would be if the sodomy laws were still on the books. However, with the U.S. Supreme Court case of *Lawrence V. Texas*, 539 U.S. 558, 2003, those laws were struck down and removed from the books."

"Thank you, Mr. Toole. This court will once again be in recess until Mr. Killam can be located," said Chief Justice Wisenrock, standing up and banging down his gavel.

"All rise," said the Bailiff as the door at the front of the courtroom once again closed.

About twenty minutes later, court reconvened.

"All rise, the Colorado State Supreme Court is now in session. The Honorable Chief Justice John Wisenrock, presiding, over the case of *Patricia Duffy-Downs et. al. v. The State of Colorado*; case number 20AP7719."

"You may be seated, and this court will come to order. I understand that this court was able to locate Mr. Killam, right?" asked Chief Justice Wisenrock, right into the speaker part of the phone.

"Yes, Your Honor, and it is wonderful to be able to speak to the high court of the State of Colorado," he said.

"Mr. Killam, were you aware that, when you prosecuted three couples on Domestic Violence charges, you put this court in an ugly legal position for their appeals case?" asked the Chief Justice, loudly.

"I wasn't aware of that, Your Honor; what am I alleged to have done wrong on their cases?" he asked, confidently.

"I will cut to the chase; you recognized and validated, on three separate occasions, same-sex marriages. You set the possible precedents that this court may have to follow," said Associate Justice Robins.

"Your Honor, same-sex couples have few, if any, true legal protections in this state. I prosecuted them because they met the requirements of the statute."

"Thank you, Mr. Killam," said the Chief Justice, hanging up the phone and looking directly to his left at Associate Justices Tartik and Hayes.

"Thanks to the prodigy you mentored years ago, Associate Justices Hayes and Tartik, this court will now have to hear the legal arguments for and against same-sex marriages. I hope that you're very smitten with yourselves," said the Chief Justice, with bile running out of the left corner of his mouth.

He turned to face the court as a whole.

"It is with the deepest of regrets that, starting tomorrow morning, this court will have to hear the arguments for and against legalizing same-sex marriages, civil unions, etc. This court will have to determine, unfortunately by error of the law, if these same-sex couples now before us in this courtroom and those similarly situated, are a protected class of citizens in this state. This court must now determine the constitutionality of the Colorado Defense of Marriage Act."

He paused for a little while to catch his breath before he continued.

"This court is now adjourned until 8:00 a.m. tomorrow morning. Mr. Fargo, it falls upon you to explain to this court why the Colorado Defense of Marriage Act is constitutional and should be upheld. You will also have to explain to this court why same-sex couples should be denied the rights, privileges and immunities reserved currently for only opposite sex couples in this state."

"Yes, Your Honor," said Mr. Fargo, solemnly.

"Mr. Marcos, you, then, have the ultimately heavy burden of proof explaining to this court why the Colorado Defense of Marriage Act is unconstitutional, and why your clients and those similarly situated in this state should have full rights," he said, banging down his gavel and standing up.

"Yes, Your Honor."

"All rise."

Daniel turned to face his clients.

"It looks like our dinner date has been postponed; I'm sorry."

"It's all right, Daniel, it will make the dinner that much more special when this is all over," said Adam.

As Daniel headed out of the courtroom, a familiar voice spoke to him.

"Dad, Tyler and I are here to fully support you," said Seth.

Daniel turned around to his left to see both of them standing there, hand in hand. They went back to the hotel after stopping by the court's daycare center to pick up Daniel's grandchildren. There were many tears of joy when Daniel told Chayton that Seth, Tyler and his cousins were in the same hotel. Daniel looked at the box that Shilah had sent him. The box contained all the Blu-ray discs that Shilah had promised him, if they were needed.

The speaker of the Senate had been on the phone with the governor. She let the governor know that she had enough loyal, unbiased and volunteer Senators at the ready for an emergency Senate confirmation of a new chief justice of the state supreme court, if it came down to it. As she was getting ready to leave for the night, Senator Lundstrom from Senate District 19 walked into her office and threw a letter down on her desktop.

"My letter of intent not to run for reelection in my Senate district this time around, you bitch! I hope you're happy!" he said as he stormed out of her office.

"Letter of intent accepted, Senator Lundstrom," said Hannah as she scratched his name off of her list and went home.

The next morning there were protestors and supporters, alike, rallying at various points around the state Supreme Court building. Once again, there was a human shield for Daniel to walk through in relative safety from his hotel room to the courthouse. After he had cleared through the even tighter security today than yesterday, he went straight to the courtroom. He then set the ten discs down on his desktop. He sat quietly with his clients and their kids. Soon, the courtroom spectator's box filled up with both supporters and protestors. The protestors stayed well away from Daniel's side of the courtroom.

Chief Justice Wisenrock was even sicker and more tired today than he had been yesterday. He had thrown up into his trashcan next to his desk many times. He was writing a very important opinion and dozing off every few minutes. He finished the opinion and went about writing a very special letter which, when he finished writing it, he put it into an envelope. When the envelope was sealed shut, Chief Justice Wisenrock put his initials across the flap. There came a knock at his chamber door; it was Associate Justice Tartik.

"Your Honor, time for court, so we can get this nonsense over with," she said, haughtily.

"I'll be out in a few minutes," replied Chief Justice Wisenrock, putting on his court robes.

Chief Justice Wisenrock entered the hallway going into his chambers and, using his badly shaking right hand, he handed the Bailiff the envelope. Chief Justice Wisenrock then whispered, hoarsely, into the Bailiff's left ear.

"Deliver that letter to the governor if anything should happen to me in court today."

"Yes, Your Honor."

The Bailiff entered the courtroom and the courtroom stood up.

"All rise, the Colorado State Supreme Court is now in session. The Honorable Chief Justice John Wisenrock, presiding, over the case of *Patricia Duffy-Downs et. al. v. The State of Colorado*; case number 20AP7719."

The justices all filed up the stairs to their respective spots on the bench.

"You may be seated and this court will come to order," said Chief Justice Wisenrock, barely now able to stand for any length of time, while banging down his gavel.

"These proceedings are being recorded and broadcast at both www.coloradocourtstv.gov\CSSC\20AP7719.htm as well as on TV channels 505, 515, 525 and 530. All of this is in accordance with the directives of the 9th Federal Circuit Court from the Proposition 8 trial. Mr. Fargo, you may begin with your opening statements."

CHAPTER 11

Mr. Fargo stood up to address the court.

"Does the state have any evidence that it wishes to enter into the court's records for the court to make an informed decision?" asked Chief Justice Wisenrock.

"No, Your Honor, I could find very little information on this current issue before the court and what information I did find was not very reliable. All I have are the wishes and concerns of some of the people in the state."

"So noted; please present your side of the case."

"Good morning, Your Honor and, if it pleases the court, the State's interest in keeping marriage to only one man and one woman is primarily to preserve and to protect the definition and institution of traditional marriage. The state further wishes to preserve and to protect a married, heterosexual couples' responsible, or irresponsible, procreation element. The state also wishes this court to uphold the rules set down in Senate bills SB15-1155, SB18-1207 and SB19-2701."

Mr. Fargo paused just long enough for Chief Justice Wisenrock to speak to him very hoarsely.

"Mr. Fargo, were you aware that Chief Judge Ulysses L. Sorensen, of the 10th Federal Circuit Court, rendered those Senate bills so named as being unconstitutional?"

"No, Your Honor, I wasn't aware of that."

"Were you also aware that he issued an emergency injunction against the enforcement in whole or in part of those Senate bills so named?"

"Again, Your Honor, I was not aware of that."

"I guess you are, now; please continue," said the Chief Justice as the courtroom chuckled a little bit.

"Thank you, Your Honor. The State wishes also to not have to change the current marriage license/certificate to include same-sex couples. This would unfairly, administratively burden the few resources that the director of the Colorado Department of Public Health and the Environment has for such things. As Your Honor is aware of, the director of the Colorado Department of Public Health and the Environment is charged with keeping these types of records as they are considered open for public viewing at any time."

Ken paused as he shuffled his notes around on his podium.

"The state legislature wishes not to have to completely rewrite Colorado Revised Statutes Titles 13, 14, 15 and 18, among others, to include same-sex couples."

"Whether or not the legislature, or any other body of the government that is subject to this court's opinion or ruling, is unfairly burdened with paperwork is a rather weak claim," said Associate Justice Robins.

"I understand, Your Honor. The director of the Colorado Department of Public Health and the Environment, who has been charged by the governor to keep the public safe from disease carrying persons, wishes to be able to keep his promise to the State to keep it as disease free as possible from the deadly, known diseases that members of the LGBTQ community possibly carry. In other words, the director wishes to keep the diseases in the LGBTQ community."

Ken looked over at Daniel and his clients before continuing.

"The State also has a duty to protect children from the LGBTQ community in that only a child raised by its biological parents is well-adjusted in society. In other words, the State wishes to keep potential child molesters from having ready access to children. Although the State allows same-sex couples to adopt and raise children, the State has only granted same-sex couples the level of Designated Beneficiaries Agreement. This is known as Colorado Revised Statutes Title 15, Article 22, Part 112. It was felt that same-sex couples should never have the same rights, privileges and immunities that are reserved exclusively for heterosexual couples.

There is evidence that same-sex couples' relationships are not as strong as a heterosexual couple's marriage or other arrangement. Same-sex couples also cannot procreate in the normal sense without the use of assistive reproductive technologies."

Ken shuffled through his notes before finishing off his arguments.

"Allowing same-sex couples full marriage rights, privileges and immunities will cause this state to see an increase in the divorce rates for years, or even decades, to come. The rate of heterosexual marriages will start dropping and there will be fewer children born. This will cause a population decrease which will hurt everyone. Further, allowing same-sex marriages to be legal, valid and recognized will destroy the very solid foundation that a traditional marriage has been based upon for several millennia; thank you, Your Honor."

Ken sat down as Daniel stood up.

"Before I launch my rebuttal to all of this garbage that has been given to the court, I would like this court to answer me two questions."

"What are those two questions, Mr. Marcos?" asked Associate Justice Smith.

"Does this court, or any court inferior to this one, have the authority to downgrade a same-sex marriage or civil union to the level of Designated Beneficiary Agreement in accordance with Colorado Revised Statutes Title 15, Article 22, Part 112? And, Your Honors, does the State of Colorado have an interest in asking gays and lesbians to change their sexual orientation or in reducing the number of gays and lesbians in the State of Colorado?"

"This court will take your questions seriously and answer them to the best of this court's abilities," said Chief Justice Wisenrock.

Daniel waited until the justices were all looking at him before he continued.

"This court challenged me to provide this court with the truth as to why the Colorado Defense of Marriage Act is unconstitutional. I will do just that and, at this time, I would like to enter into the court's records these ten Blu-ray discs," said Daniel, offering them to the Bailiff, who then handed them to Chief Justice Wisenrock.

"Objection, Your Honor, I must, for the sake of protecting the State's interests in this case, place a blanket objection to the submission of this evidence."

"Your objection is noted and overruled. This court gave you plenty of opportunity to present evidence to support your statements and nothing concrete was ever entered into the court's records," said Chief Justice Wisenrock.

"Thank you, Your Honor. I will present my evidence in five sections. I will start out with the historical impact issues first before moving on to the constitutional impact issues. I will then move into the economic, personal and religious impact issues."

"How long will this all take, Mr. Marcos?" asked Chief Justice Wisenrock as he started dozing off again.

"Probably the rest of the day and all of my evidence is on those discs for the court to review as many times as necessary. The evidence includes names, addresses, phone numbers, fax numbers, email addresses, etc."

"I see; can you start this at 1:00 p.m.?" asked Chief Justice Wisenrock.

"I certainly can, Your Honor."

"Good, this court is in recess until 1:00 p.m.," said Chief Justice Wisenrock, standing up and banging down his gavel. The justices all filed out of the courtroom as, outside the courthouse, the protestors were starting to get ugly with the police. The supporters were doing their best not to start or get involved in a riot, but the police were waiting in full riot gear. After lunch, Daniel returned to the courtroom after clearing through even more tight security than this morning. The Bailiff stood up as did the rest of the courtroom as the justices all filed in.

"All rise, the Colorado State Supreme Court is now in session. The Honorable Chief Justice John Wisenrock, presiding, over the case of *Patricia Duffy-Downs et. al. v. The State of Colorado*; case number 20AP7719."

"You may be seated and this court will come to order," said Chief Justice Wisenrock, banging down his gavel and taking his seat at the bench.

"These proceedings are being recorded and broadcast at both www.coloradocourtstv.gov\CSSC\20AP7719.htm as well as on TV channels 505, 515, 525 and 530. All of this is in accordance with the directives of the 9th Federal Circuit Court from the Proposition 8 trial. You may begin, Mr. Marcos," said Chief Justice Wisenrock, weakly this time.

"Thank you, Your Honor. Good afternoon and, if it pleases the court, I will start presenting evidence to counter my esteemed colleague's arguments. I will first start off with the historical impact issues because I want this court to know where this whole LGBTQ movement started. I also want the court to have the truth so that the court can make a good, legally-based, decision."

"Proceed, Mr. Marcos and get this farce over with and quit wasting the court's time," said Associate Justice Tartik.

"I will do as you wish, Your Honor. The entire LGBTQ movement can be traced to one single incident; the Stonewall Riots started the LGBTQ movement June 28th, 1969 in New York City. New York City subsequently held its first gay Pridefest in 1977. The LGBTQ movement has yet to be stopped."

Daniel paused before going on since it appeared he had several of associate justices' attention.

"Traditional Marriages, Your Honors? Let me see, how about single moms who never marry and are raising kids without their fathers around. Let's add gold diggers, aunts, and uncles and grandparents who are raising the kids because the parents are in prison, divorced or they have no time for the kids. Let's also add to that list, celebrities; they are great role models for a traditional marriage. I forgot to add heterosexual couples who never marry. The list is much longer than this, but it is all I can say before it makes me so mad I can't see straight."

There was a slight chuckle from both the bench and the courtroom. Chief Justice Wisenrock smiled and banged his gavel down so that Daniel could continue his speech.

"Responsible or irresponsible procreation was brought up by my esteemed colleague. Let's take a look at that argument in one event; the first test tube baby was born July 25th, 1978. She is happily married and has kids of her own. Now, let's move on to the year 1989. In 1989, two gay men, who were superstars of the time, set the world on fire by marrying in the State of California. Sadly, because of the fanfare from their high profile marriage, it came to an end around July 18th, 1996. Their same-sex marriage did prove that two people of the same-sex could have a long lasting and loving relationship."

Daniel had to pause while he looked over his notes before he continued.

"In 1995, the State of California passed the toughest and only anti-discrimination laws in the United States. They modeled theirs after the Israeli one passed a few years earlier. California Revised Statutes Civil Law Title 10620, Section 51 of the Civil Code, referred to as the Unruh Civil Rights Act, made equal rights for all the law with stiff penalties for violating them. Now, let's move to the year 2007. On June 2, 2007, California becomes the only state to allow inmates who have same-sex partners/same-sex marriages, civil unions or domestic partnerships the right to stay overnight with their mates."

"Mr. Marcos, I don't believe you that California allows same-sex overnight visits," said Associate Justice Tartik.

"They do, Your Honor and a copy of the decree signed by the governor of the State of California is on those discs for your viewing," replied Daniel.

He paused once again.

"On June 12, 2007, forty years after the landmark U.S. Supreme Court ruling, Mrs. Loving made her last statement to the world about the *Loving V. Virginia* case, 388 U.S. 1, 1967. She stated to the world that, 'No one should be denied the right to marry the person they love because of their race, creed, national origin or sexual orientation.' Strange, that the State of Colorado abolished its miscegenation laws in 1957 under House Bill HB-1039, a full ten years before the Loving ruling. Yet, the voters passed a miscegenation law about fifty years later."

Daniel saw the pens of all the justices going furiously for several minutes. This gave Daniel time to conclude this part of the historical impact issues.

"Let's move on to the State of Colorado for that same year. On December 9, 2007, a crazed gunman opened fire on church patrons at the Good News Church in Monument, Colorado. The female security officer, Debbie Reins, returned fire killing the gunman. She is present in this courtroom, Your Honors, along with her wife of fourteen years; is that right?" asked Daniel as he looked behind him to see her standing up with her wife before sitting back down.

"She was treated as a hero by the church, the media and the community. When she brought her wife to one of the services a few weeks later, she was told to leave and not to come back ever again. Nice way to treat someone who put into practice, unconditional love and unconditional acceptance of others along with being willing to sacrifice themselves for others. 1 Corinthians 13: 4-7 and John 15:13, am I right, Associate Justice Tartik and Associate Justice Hayes?"

This made both of them squirm uneasily in their chairs.

"Now, let's continue with the State of Colorado and a point brought up by my esteemed colleague about child molesters. I would like the court to take a look at the Belfour Study conducted in the State of Colorado's penal system beginning January 1st, 2017 and running through December 31st, 2017. The study followed one hundred sex offenders, specifically, those who played around with little boys and girls. Ninety-eight identified themselves as straight; of those, seventy-five were married with kids or grandkids of their own. Forty of them were Caucasian, twenty African American, twenty Hispanics, five American Samoans, five Pacific Islanders and eight American Eskimos. One African American identified himself as bisexual and one identified himself a gay Native American affiliated with the Ute Nation here in Colorado. The full results of the Belfour Study can be found at www.belfourstudy.org."

Daniel saw the pens going once again and waited patiently for them to stop before he went on.

"Here are some more issues brought up by Mr. Fargo. Fifteen states in 2021 now allow same-sex marriages. Why not completely prohibit them if they are so bad? In those states that still have their Defense of Marriage Acts intact, their respective legislatures' have enacted laws that specifically prohibit same-sex marriages and they make it a crime to perform a same-sex marriage in at least twenty-two of the thirty-five states. If you move to one of those twenty-two states and have a same-sex marriage license, you could be arrested and convicted of violating the law in those twenty-two states. The fine, on average in those twenty-two states, is a night in jail or a $500 fine or both. None of those states have EVER required a church or other religious entity to recognize a same-sex marriage, especially if the church or other religious entity objects to the same-sex marriage."

Daniel smiled as he looked at a very nervous Mr. Fargo.

"In those same fifteen states, the divorce rates, based upon a fifteen year previous history, have remained unchanged by legalizing same-sex marriages with the exception of the State of Massachusetts. The first year after their state Supreme Court legalized same-sex marriages, the divorce rate spiked; going from 3.2% to 3.3%. Divorce rates were unchanged in the other ten states after same-sex marriages were legalized. Also in those fifteen states, the traditional marriage rates have remained unchanged from the previous fifteen years when same-sex marriages were illegal, prohibited or not valid or recognized. The only exception was the State of Kansas where the first year after they legalized same-sex marriages, the traditional marriage rate spiked going from 2.9% to 3.0%."

Daniel looked down at his notes once again to make sure he completed the first section before moving on to the next section.

"And finally, Your Honor, when genealogists look to put together a family history or tree, they search birth and death records as well as marriage licenses. All of these items are available from the Bureau of Vital Statistics or the Department of Public Health and the Environment to anyone wishing to establish their heritage."

Chief Justice Wisenrock stood up and looked down at Daniel.

"This court will be in recess for twenty minutes," he said, banging down his gavel as they all left the courtroom.

"All rise."

When the justices were once again ready, the Bailiff stood up as did the rest of the courtroom.

"All rise, the Colorado State Supreme Court is now in session. The Honorable Chief Justice John Wisenrock presiding over the case of *Patricia Duffy-Downs et. al. v. The State of Colorado*; case number 20AP7719."

"You may be seated and this court will come to order; Mr. Marcos you may continue," said Chief Justice Wisenrock, banging down his gavel.

"Thank you, Your Honor and I will now move into the constitutional impact issues."

"Did you vote for or against the Defense of Marriage Act when it was on the ballot?" asked Associate Justice Hale.

"I voted against it, Your Honor, because the Defense of Marriage Act is unconstitutional for many reasons, which I will be going over. My colleague here brought up the Disher case several times. This case is not even close to being similar to the *People V. Disher* 224 P.3D 254. We are once again going down the same path as this state did in *Romer V. Evans* 517 U.S. 620, 1996."

He shuffled through this part of his notes before going on.

"Many people have brought up the issue of civil unions as an alternative to marriage for members of the LGBTQ community; let me give this court the legal definition of a civil union. In the context of family law, a civil union is a marriage-like relationship, often between members of the same sex, recognized by civil authorities within a jurisdiction. Civil unions are also known as civil partnerships."

Seeing more pen movements on the bench, Daniel waited until they stopped before continuing.

"The Defense of Marriage Act is also unconstitutional in that, as it is worded in Colorado Revised Statutes, Title 14, Article 2, Part 110, it is an Ex Post Facto law."

"How is that possible, Mr. Marcos?" asked Associate Justice Smith, trying to sit up as far as she could to hear Daniel's answer.

"Your Honor, simply put, a marriage is nothing more than a civil contract between two people, essentially. The Defense of Marriage Act violates Article I, Section 10, of the U.S. Constitution with respect to the Ex Post Facto Law and Breach of Contract wording. In 2018, the Colorado Legislature passed and the then governor signed into law Senate Bill SB18-0900 making breach of contract a criminal only offense; therefore it falls under the ex post facto law test."

"Are you aware of any U.S. Supreme Court or lower court cases dealing with an Ex Post Facto Law?" asked Associate Justice Kathryn.

"Yes, the only Ex Post Facto Law court case was *Calder V. Bull*, 1798, case number 3 U.S. 386. The court ruled that Ex Post Facto laws didn't apply to civil law, but only to criminal law as intended by the Founding Fathers."

He waited to see if there were any more questions; after a few minutes, he saw the pens stop and he continued.

"The Defense of Marriage Act is also unconstitutional under Article IV, Section 1 of the U.S. Constitution, applies as well in reference to the Defense of Marriage Act and the 14th Amendment, Section 1, applies as well in reference to the Defense of Marriage Act."

He paused, this time more for himself than the justices.

"Now, let me give you some further information to consider. Twenty years after Loving V. Virginia, in 1987, the U.S. Supreme Court ruled in *Turner V. Safely*, 482 U.S. 78 that, even if you are incarcerated and cannot consummate the marriage or even procreate, you have the right to get married; nobody has the authority to stop even an inmate from marrying."

He didn't wait this time for the pens to stop writing, he went ahead.

"In 1988, the U.S. Supreme Court case of *Bowers V. Hardwick* 478 U.S. 186 abolished only the sodomy laws in the State of Georgia. Yet, Israel did the same thing for the entire country a year earlier. The Defense of Marriage Act also meets the requirements of a miscegenation law in that no matter what race my clients are, they can't get married."

"Mr. Marcos, those laws were stricken from the books with the Loving ruling in 1967," said Associate Justice Robins.

"Not entirely correct, Your Honor. In 1998, thirty-one years after the Loving case, the State of Alabama still prosecuted people for violating their miscegenation laws. Your mother and father lived in South Carolina didn't they?"

"Yes, but what has that got to do with this case?" he asked in return.

"In 2000, thirty-three years after the Loving case, the State of South Carolina still prosecuted people for violating their miscegenation laws. It wouldn't be until June 26th, 2003, when all of the sodomy laws that were still on the books, including the ones on the books for the State of Colorado, were struck down by the

United States Supreme Court in the *Lawrence V. Texas* case, 539 U.S. 558."

Associate Justice Robins sat back in his chair.

"Now, let's move to the year 2006. In 2006, the Colorado Defense of Marriage Act was passed. This act, referred by the voters as ballot initiative Amendment 45, clearly violates Article II, Section 29 of the Colorado Constitution. It also creates a protected class of citizens who cannot be prosecuted for a certain crime because their intimate relationship doesn't exist in the eyes of the law."

He shuffled through his notes to make sure that he was still on track to completing this segment.

"We now come to the great State of California and a direct challenge in both their state supreme court and the 9th Federal Circuit Court to their Defense of Marriage Act brought about because of the state's anti-discrimination law. At the Proposition 8 Trial in the 9th Federal Circuit Court, the California State Attorney General at the time was asked about the constitutionality of the Proposition 8 ballot initiative by the chief judge hearing the case. He replied to the court in writing via memorandum, 'Proposition 8 is unconstitutional under California Civil Law, Section 10620; the Unruh Civil Rights Act. To answer the court's other question; I do not have the duty, right or privilege of stopping a ballot initiative from being placed on the ballot even if I know that the ballot initiative, after carefully reviewing it, is unconstitutional . . . '"

Daniel waited so that the pens would stop once again.

"Let's move up to the federal government level. In 2011, the U.S. Attorney General issued a memorandum to all of the lower district court attorney generals, after a meeting with the President of the United States at that time, stating that the federal Defense of Marriage Act is unconstitutional and not to defend it in court if the law is challenged; memo number 20110223. They cited violations of the 9th Amendment, the 14th Amendment and Article IV, Section 1 as reasons."

Daniel stopped for several minutes to gather his thoughts on the final section of this part of the issue.

"To close on this part of the subject, Your Honors, Domestic Partnerships and Civil Unions do not meet the requirements of equal rights for all granted by both the federal and state constitutions. 'Separate but equal has never been in our society . . .' *Brown V. Board of Education Topeka, Kansas et. al.* 347 U.S. 483, 1954. I also ask Your Honors to look at *Craig V. Boren* 429 U.S. 190, 1976, *Massachusetts Board of Retirement V. Murgia*, 427 U.S. 307, 1976 and *Goodridge V. Massachusetts Department of Public Health* for my clients' sake and those who are similarly situated when rendering your decision."

"Was there any attempt by the legislature to make same-sex marriages illegal before the adoption of the Defense of Marriage Act, that you know of, Mr. Marcos?" asked Associate Justice Hale.

"Yes, Your Honor. House Bill HB96-1291 would have added to the prohibited marriages statute of Colorado Revised Statues Section 1, paragraph D. This failed to be veto overridden in 1996, garnering only 28% of the required 66% vote of the full state legislature."

"This court will take another twenty minute recess," said Chief Justice Wisenrock as he feebly banged down his gavel.

"All rise."

Court was soon back in session for the conclusion of the case.

"All rise, the Colorado State Supreme Court is now in session. The Honorable Chief Justice John Wisenrock, presiding, over the case of *Patricia Duffy-Downs et. al. v. The State of Colorado*; case number 20AP7719."

"You may be seated and this court will come to order. Mr. Marcos, please continue with your case," said Chief Justice Wisenrock, banging down his gavel, weakly, once again and sitting down very hard into his chair.

"Thank you, Your Honor and I will now move into the economic impact issues of the Defense of Marriage Act. In 2000, the City of Colorado Springs decided to discontinue the benefits for its city employees for their same-sex partners. This also cost the City of Colorado Springs and El Paso County millions of dollars in lost revenue."

"How, Mr. Marcos?" asked Associate Justice Tartik.

"On December 4, 2000, Kelsten Airlines was to come to the city to provide thousands of jobs with a heavy aircraft maintenance facility. Kelsten Airlines pulled out when their executives saw the newspaper headlines that morning. They came to Denver because of what the City of Colorado Springs had done to its employees. Kelsten Airlines is one of the 303 Fortune 500 companies that grant full benefits to their same-sex partnered employees. These benefits are established by same-sex marriage licenses, Civil Union certificates or Domestic Partnership paperwork. The hate and animosity is clear in the El Paso County area."

Associate Justices Tartik and Hayes sat up when they heard that statement.

"I would like the court to take judicial notice of the fact that out of the 303 Fortune 500 companies, prior to the adoption of DOMA in the State of Colorado, fifty-five of those 303 companies called Colorado their headquarters. As of this year, 2021, only three are left. The State of Colorado's State Treasurer estimates, due to the lack of actual physical data that, since the passage of DOMA, DOMA has cost over 500,000 people to lose their jobs in this state alone. The State Treasurer estimates, again, due to lack of actual physical data, that the State of Colorado has lost more than $900,000.00 per year for the past 15 years. To put that into perspective, that amounts to over $13,500,000.00 in lost income tax and corporate business tax revenues which the state receives a lot of from companies."

He waited before putting out the next fact.

"Here's another economic fact; The Colorado Department of Revenue estimates that since the Defense of Marriage Act was passed, the state has lost almost half a billion dollars in revenue every year. This estimated loss of revenue comes from such sources as hotel taxes, food taxes, entertainment taxes, parking fees, etc."

Daniel had to shuffle his cards around while the pens were still going; when they stopped, he went on.

"My esteemed colleague brought up the administrative costs of legalizing same-sex marriages. The Colorado Department of Public Health and the Environment, who issues marriage licenses in the State of Colorado, concedes that there doesn't seem to be any disastrous results from issuing same-sex marriage licenses to same-sex couples as the marriage license itself hardly changes at all. The only change on the form is where it says Bride and

Groom; it will now have to say Bride A and Bride B or Groom A and Groom B."

Daniel stopped so that the pens could catch up.

"The cost of the marriage license will generate much needed revenue for the state and there doesn't seem to be any indication that issuing of the licenses will cause a stampede to the marriage license offices. A marriage license can be downloaded off of the internet, filled in and printed up all at the same time with the effort and cost of the person wishing to download said document. When they file their marriage license, they have to pay the administrative filing fee for the respective county clerk and recorder. Again, it generates revenue for the county and the state."

"Then, I surmise, you have seen a same-sex marriage license, Mr. Marcos?" asked Associate Justice Smith.

"Yes, Your Honor, I have seen several. My esteemed colleague brought up the fact that same-sex couples can adopt in this state. He didn't tell you all of the provisions of an adoption like that, Your Honor; here's the truth. The Colorado Child Adoption Agency, herein referred to as the CCAA, requires same-sex couples, who wish to adopt a child or more than one child if they can afford to do such a thing, to take twenty-seven MANDATORY classes ranging from child rearing and parenting to discipline and behavior problems, etc. The cost for these twenty-seven classes is about $9,000.00 and must be completed BEFORE the CCAA will complete the adoption process. In contrast, a heterosexual couple, wishing to do the same adoption or adoptions, is only required to take five of those same twenty-seven mandatory classes that same-sex couples have to take, at a nominal cost of only $1,000.00. The other twenty-two classes are OPTIONAL for heterosexual couples."

He was shuffling through his cards again when Associate Justice Kathryn spoke.

"Mr. Marcos, you stated earlier in your testimony that the State of California has an anti-discrimination law; is there a copy of that law available to this court?" he asked.

"Yes, there is, Your Honor, on disc number three."

"Thank you."

"Anytime, Your Honor. Now, I will start getting into the personal impact issues of the Defense of Marriage Act."

Daniel paused so that Chief Justice Wisenrock could throw up into one of the trashcans near him. When Chief Justice Wisenrock had returned to the upright position in his chair, Daniel continued.

"Let's start out in the year 1999 in the city of Colorado Springs. In 1999, the Colorado Springs Fire Department sent their best representative to the International Police and Fire Games; Holly French. She brought back a VERY coveted trophy being officially designated the "Fittest Female Firefighter in the World." This was her second trophy of that type. Her first trophy was being designated the "Fittest Female in the U.S. Army" in the early 1990's. She was very proud of that trophy and honor as well as the first trophy she won, but she is also a lesbian."

Daniel shuffled through his note cards once again to make sure that he was still on track.

"My esteemed colleague here brought up health issues; let me give this court the truthful data on that issue. Data from the previous twenty years in those fifteen states, from the Centers for Disease Control, indicates that the reported number of HIV/AIDS cases, Hepatitis cases and HPV cases have either dropped or remained unchanged in the LGBTQ community. Sadly, the number of those same diseases for the heterosexual community in those fifteen states for the same twenty year period has risen by a sum total of 300%."

All the justices were looking at Daniel closely.

"I now understand from a former client, Dr. Lazlo, who is present in this courtroom, that he has received tentative approval for HIV vaccine testing on humans from the U.S. Food and Drug Administration. Let's look at some other health issues since we are on that subject. In the late 1990's, despite trying to keep the findings from being published in the medical world, doctors discovered that gay and bisexual males don't develop prostate cancer at the extremely high rates of their heterosexual male counterparts. Granted, a gay or bisexual man can still get prostate cancer, but it is rare for them."

Daniel then turned to face Mr. Fargo while addressing another, more personal, issue.

"Your Honor, my colleague here brought up to me the issue of cheating in the LGBTQ community. Cheating does occur in the LGBTQ community, but it is rare in that unlike an unwanted pregnancy, divorce, alimony payments, child support payments, etc., cheating in the LGBTQ community may mean a death sentence to both parties. This seems to keep the LGBTQ community a little more responsible for their actions."

Daniel turned to face Seth and Tyler. Daniel motioned for them to stand up, and they did, holding hands like any other couple that is in love would do. Daniel prayed that Seth would say the right words in the right tone of voice for the court just like they had practiced in the hotel room earlier that morning.

"Now, Your Honor, I would like this court to hear from my son and his husband on how the Defense of Marriage Act has affected them."

Seth cleared his throat in order to speak clearly.

"Good afternoon, Your Honor, and I doubt you will remember me."

"Seth, I may be very ill, but I do remember you being in this courtroom along with your father and so do Associate Justices Hale and Smith. You had just lost your mother, and you had to have your appendix removed. I believe you were in this courtroom over the issue of possible evidence on your cell phone. I also seem to recall that you later took on your high school principal and the school district in federal court, winning your case."

"Yes, Your Honor, I did win my case and someone obviously has done their homework on me. Before I begin speaking directly to you as the court, I would like to play a short, ten minute DVD about where Tyler, I and our twin boys live, work and play."

"By all means," said Chief Justice Wisenrock.

The DVD was put into the DVD player and everyone watched the video. When it was over, there was a certain sense of calmness in the courtroom which was just what Seth had hoped would happen.

"Now, Your Honor, dolphins are not stupid mammals; they are very capable of determining character from just a few minutes with you in the water. Believe me when I tell you, they can see straight into your soul and can tell if you are true to yourself or not; you can't fool them."

The plan was working just like Daniel said it would. This made Seth a little more relaxed and increased his confidence.

"Teko, Meko, Kyushu and Migo are all hermaphrodite dolphins who live in the waters surrounding the Caribbean Island where my husband and I live and work. Because they are hermaphrodites, their pods rejected them. They are all relatively young dolphins at what I estimate is forty-five years of age. We also have twin boys who keep us very busy."

Seth had finally started to loosen his grip on Tyler's left hand. Tyler was very thankful for that since the feeling had long since left his left hand.

"These dolphins, because we treated them for their various injuries and illnesses and treated them with unconditional love and unconditional acceptance, have adopted me, my husband and the twin boys as their "pod." Now, before anyone gets overly excited about this "family" arrangement, those are very much wild dolphins that are free to come and go as they please. We have no hold over them of any kind, and we all know that one day they could leave and never come back."

Seth saw the pens writing as fast as they could go and waited until the last pen had been put down before continuing.

"I would like the court to take judicial notice of the fact that dolphins are the only other mammals on this planet that will actively seek out a human for companionship. Dolphins are also the only other mammal on this planet, besides humans, that has sex for pleasure as well as reproduction. Dolphins are very long lived, reaching between eighty to one hundred years old in the wild and up to one hundred and twenty years old in captivity."

"Mr. Thompson-Marcos, you don't have to use such legal terms," said Chief Justice Wisenrock, smiling at him.

"I was told by my father to use such terms so that the court would not lose interest in the information being given."

"A very admirable trait; please continue and, yes, this court will take judicial notice of what you have to say," said Chief Justice Wisenrock, with more energy now than ever.

"Thank you, Your Honor. On the other side of the island, we live in a large beach house left behind by some pirates in the 18th century. This private beach house has access to a nice sandy beach along with a large lagoon. Anytime my husband, the twin boys or I go for a swim in the lagoon, no matter what time of the day or night, the dolphins show up a little while later. They know us that well so they will show up no matter where they are swimming around at the island."

Seth had to pause before going on since he was starting to sweat a little from the concentration it took to complete this speech.

"A few months ago, while we were all swimming in the lagoon, my twin boys started to drown. As a parent, I had to think the worst, but Teko and Migo didn't let them drown. Instead, they pushed them towards the small dock and kept their heads above water. Those dolphins could have let them drown, and there would be two less humans on the planet because there was no way for me to get out to them in time. To say the least, it was a very scary situation. After that incident, I started to learn how to ride the dolphins and eventually taught the boys and my husband how to ride them. Thank you, Your Honor, for taking the time to listen to what was said."

Everyone in the spectator's box started clapping and whistling before Chief Justice Wisenrock started banging his gavel down to restore order. When order had been finally reestablished, Chief Justice Wisenrock called for a one hour break. Daniel waited patiently with his clients and noticed that the sun was starting to set already. The Bailiff stood up as did the rest of the court.

"All rise, the Colorado State Supreme Court is now in session. The Honorable Chief Justice John Wisenrock, presiding, over the case of *Patricia Duffy-Downs et. al. v. The State of Colorado*; case number 20AP7719."

"You may be seated and this court will come to order. Mr. Marcos, you may proceed," said Chief Justice Wisenrock, who was now turning even more ashen white with every passing minute.

"Thank you, Your Honor. I will now conclude this journey with the religious impact issues. If any of you associate justices don't want to hear what I have to say, you may leave."

Since none of the associate justices left the courtroom, Daniel took that as a sign to go ahead.

"I would like to have the court take judicial notice of the fact that Israel is the birth place of more than thirty religions across the globe. We are now going to move on to the most talked about and, perhaps, misunderstood, passages out of the Bible; they are the Bible passages out of the Book of Leviticus 18:22 and Leviticus 20:13."

Daniel paused before continuing.

"Leviticus 18 verse 22, 'Homosexuality is absolutely forbidden, for it is an enormous sin.' Leviticus 20 verse 13, 'The penalty for homosexual acts is death to both parties. They have brought it upon themselves.' Most members of the LGBTQ community were born that way; it is NOT a choice they made and, if being the way they are offends the Creator, why has He not brought about Armageddon? Interestingly, the Book of Leviticus was written for the priests and the Levites, hence its namesake."

This time Daniel only waited a short time because a little voice in the back of his mind told him that the chief justice didn't have much longer to live.

"My colleague here brought up child rearing; simply put, Your Honor, there is NO concrete, scientific evidence that proves a same-sex couple is any worse off raising children that are well-adjusted than a heterosexual couple. The only thing that hurts the children in a same-sex marriage is not to have the marriage recognized or validated by the state in which they reside. In other words, a same-sex couple's children are no better than or worse off than those of their heterosexual counterparts. The family structure is essentially the same and the dynamics of the family structure are essentially the same."

He moved quickly once again, feeling the pressure in the courtroom that time was running out for him and his clients.

"Israel abolished all Sodomy Laws in 1987. In 1992, Israel passed the toughest anti-discrimination laws in the world to include the protections for those LGBTQ Israeli citizens in housing and employment. This anti-discrimination law includes SEVERE penalties for committing acts of violence against Israeli LGBTQ citizens to include the death penalty. In 1993, Israel allowed LGBTQ military members to openly serve. That same year, on December 21, President Bill Clinton signed into law the "Don't Ask, Don't Tell" policy preventing LGBTQ members from openly serving for the U.S. Military."

Chief Justice Wisenrock started throwing up in a trashcan once again, so Daniel paused until he was done.

"On June 28, 2002, the Israeli government granted permission to allow its first gay Pridefest to be held in Jerusalem. Although the Israeli military was on full alert for the possibility of trouble, no trouble materialized. In 2004, the Israeli Supreme Court ruled that LGBTQ couples qualify for both common law marriage and full inheritance rights. In 2005, the Israeli Supreme Court granted full adoption rights for LGBTQ Israeli couples. In 2006, Israel recognized same-sex marriages performed in other countries."

"Mr. Marcos, Denver holds a Pridefest each year," said Associate Justice Tartik.

"You're right, Your Honor. Pridefests are also held in Colorado Springs, under the threat of a lawsuit for civil rights violations if the permit is denied, and in Boulder and Pueblo. On March 18, 2010, a Justice of the Peace in the State of Louisiana refused to marry an interracial couple because he felt the miscegenation laws should not have been struck down by the U.S. Supreme Court."

"Are you serious, Mr. Marcos?" asked a very perplexed Associate Justice Vince Kathryn.

"I am dead serious about it, Your Honor. The news article is on disc five, I believe. Now, let's jump ahead to the year 2012. In March of 2012, a simple high school yearbook photo caused a mass outcry of hate and animosity towards the yearbook staff, the school, and the lesbian couple. The yearbook staff was ordered, "Pull that picture or the yearbook doesn't get printed . . ." by one of the large contingent of church leaders within El Paso County. Censorship is obviously run with an iron fist despite the 1st Amendment protections for the media."

Daniel had to wait again while Chief Justice Wisenrock took care of business with another trashcan.

"Here are some more facts about how destructive religion can be to a governmental body. In the 20th Century alone, because of religion getting too deep into the thought processes of governments, 56,000,000 people were rounded up and slaughtered by their respective governments. Whether you were Jewish, Kurdish, Christian or whatever, you were a religious threat to the government and, therefore, you must be eliminated as a religious threat. Here are some familiar names of world leaders who slaughtered their own people over religious views contrary to the governments: Slobodan Milosevic, Adolf Hitler, Joseph Stalin, Saddam Hussein and Idi Amin to name just a few."

"That's getting a bit harsh, isn't it, Mr. Marcos?" asked Associate Justice Hayes.

"No, and the list gets better, Your Honor. In the 21st century, unless something is done to stop it, that number, because of religion, will be almost twice that of the 20th Century. Let me put the number into prospective for you. 56,000,000 people is the sum total of the top nine most populous states here in the United States. That's nine states full of people that were wiped out by their respective governments over religion."

The justices were all uncomfortable with the religious aspect that Daniel was discussing as they were all squirming around in their chairs.

"For you, Associate Justice Tartik and Associate Justice Hayes, think about this chapter and verse carefully before rendering your decision. "Judge not others as you shall be judged yourself just as harshly." Words to that affect come from Matthew 7:1. I would like to give the court my closing statements."

"Proceed," said Chief Justice Wisenrock, with his eyes rolling back into his head a little.

"Thank you, Your Honors, for taking the time to hear this case. I want the court to remember this when rendering its decision."

"What exactly is that, Mr. Marcos, since you seem to be able to waste this court's time on such a farce as this," snapped Associate Justice Hayes.

"In closing, Your Honors, I want this court to take judicial notice of the fact that since this country's founding, 1,248,848 men and women have given their lives to defend Her; 624,511 during the Civil War, all over the color of someone's skin. They were property that could be bought, sold, and taxed accordingly just like me. Your Honors, let us not forget that at one time I was taxed as

3/5 of a person before the Civil War and the passage of the 14th Amendment. I also want this court not to forget the words that are on the front of this building, 'Liberty and justice for all.' My clients and those similarly situated received no liberty and no justice in this state. I also want this court to remember these words as well, 'We the People of the United States' and 'We the People of the State of Colorado.'" Those words, Your Honors, mean everyone, not just a select few. They either apply to all, or they mean nothing."

He paused before continuing.

"I would like the court to take judicial notice of what is guaranteed by the U.S. Constitution, Article IV, Section IV. We are guaranteed a Republic form of government. I would like to refresh the court's memory on what a Republic form of government is: A sovereign state in which supreme power is held by the people and their elected Representatives; which also has a President versus a monarch. We sometimes forget that in our hurried ways of doing things in our very complicated lives that we have today."

"Thank you, Mr. Marcos, for educating this court and the people of the State of Colorado with the truth. We shall render a verdict in either late August or early September, but I wish to thank you personally for everything," said Chief Justice Wisenrock as he walked down to shake Daniel's left hand.

As he shook Daniel's left hand, his eyes suddenly widened as if in terrible pain or terror, Daniel couldn't tell which one. Chief Justice Wisenrock then convulsed and threw-up huge amounts of blood onto Daniel as Chief Justice Wisenrock collapsed to the floor. As cameras flashed, Daniel gently lowered Chief Justice Wisenrock to the floor.

In the crowd, Chief Justice Wisenrock's personal physician stepped forward, fighting his way to the fallen judge. He then flashed a light into both of the justice's eyes a few times. He looked up at the paramedics coming in the side doors to the courtroom and shook his head.

"He's gone, there's nothing anyone can do for him. I am sorry, Mr. Marcos, that he did that to you," said the doctor as one of the paramedics handed Daniel a bio-hazard bag. Daniel looked over at his clients with tears in his eyes as they loaded Chief Justice Wisenrock's body onto the gurney. During this whole melee`, the

Bailiff had left the courtroom to deliver the letter to the governor as instructed. The Bailiff returned to the nightmarish scene in the courtroom.

"I think it's over for our case; I am truly sorry," said Daniel, with more tears in his eyes.

"You did your best, and that is all we expected you to do; come to dinner, and bring your family and friends," said Adam.

Seth stepped forward.

"I'll go get a change of clothes for you, Dad."

"Thank you, Seth. Is there any way I can get cleaned up by the time he returns, Bailiff? I don't think walking around downtown Denver with blood all over me is a good idea right now."

When Seth showed up with Daniel's change of clothes, the only people in the courtroom were Daniel, Tyler and some news reporters.

"I'm sorry for you and your clients, Mr. Marcos and, if that bitch Associate Justice Tartik takes over, I will quit," said the Bailiff.

"I truly understand your frustration, Bailiff," replied a somber Daniel, taking his change of clothes from Seth.

"Mr. Marcos, let me lock up the courtroom here and you can take a shower downstairs in the employee locker room. I will let you borrow my shampoo and conditioner. There are soap dispensers in the shower area for you to use."

"That's very kind of you, Bailiff, and thank you very much."

The governor had watched the whole thing on TV in his office. He picked up the phone and called the State Attorney General Sam Toole at home.

"Did you see what I saw on TV in the courtroom of the state supreme court?" asked the governor.

"Yes, and I am not entirely certain that court is over."

"What makes you think that, Sam?"

"I never heard the gavel bang down. I also never heard him say court is over, adjourned, postponed, or continued to a future date."

"You know, come to think of it, I didn't hear anything like that said, either. So, what you're telling me is, for the first time in the court's 144 year history, the chief justice died in open court without properly closing the court records? This is going to be one really messy legal nightmare."

"I must agree with you on that one."

"Well, now I have another legal question for you."

"Go ahead."

"What is the legal validity of a deathbed confession?"

"Generally speaking, a deathbed confession is a legally binding statement that every court in the fifty states, U.S. Protectorates and Territories, as well as the District of Columbia, recognizes as being valid testimony in a court case."

"Could a deathbed confession be challenged in a court of law on the basis that the person giving the confession or statement was possibly mentally unstable due to sickness or injury?"

"To the best of my knowledge, no deathbed confession or statement has ever been denied the weight of evidence in a court of law. To the best of my knowledge, no court of law has ever denied a deathbed confession or statement on the basis of the person's mental status regardless of sickness or injury. The only legal requirement of a deathbed confession or statement is that the person giving the confession or statement knows or reasonably knows that they are going to or about to die."

"I see; I guess we will have to cross that bridge when, or if, we ever come to it. What about appointing a new chief justice, even if it is for a short period of time?"

"You can, because of the executive powers granted to you by both the Colorado Constitution and the legislature, designate whoever you want as the replacement."

"Do I need confirmation from anyone to do this temporary appointment?"

"No, you would only need to do that if the legislature was still in session; since that is an area exclusive to the Speaker of the Senate, I would call her."

"Thank you; goodbye."

The governor called the Speaker of the Senate at her home, first. When the governor was told that she was enroute to the Capitol Building, he called her in her chambers.

"I surmise that you saw what happened on TV about an hour ago, now?"

"Yes, and I was prepared, as I discussed with you earlier, with a plan for this type of issue."

"Put the plan into immediate operation."

"I already have; the last of the volunteer Senators should arrive at the Capitol Building within the hour. Do you have anyone in mind for this emergency Senate confirmation hearing?"

"Mr. Daniel Marcos."

"Good choice, Your Honor; goodbye."

"Thank you, Madam Speaker; goodbye," said the governor, hanging up the phone. The governor then wrote something down on a piece of stationary which he put into the same envelope as the original letter.

He made a copy of the letter that he had received from the Supreme Court Bailiff earlier. He put both copies into an envelope and sealed it up. He hand delivered the envelope to the speaker of the Senate. She opened up the letter after the governor had left and followed the instructions that had been written down. The Sergeant-At-Arms was busy making all of the arrangements for the late night hearing. The governor went to his home instead of his office where he spoke to his executive security staff.

"I don't care how many cops, badges, guns, helicopters and dogs it takes, but find Mr. Daniel Marcos. When you find him, bring him to the Capitol Building immediately and make sure that he gets to the Senate chambers."

"Yes, sir," said the man as he started talking rapidly into his cell phone.

Within an hour, law enforcement had secured the floor of the hotel that Daniel was staying in; no one was getting on the floor that didn't have a room there. The governor returned to the Capitol Building to address the people of the State of Colorado via the news. The governor was standing on a step of the Capitol Building. A makeshift podium had been set up for the public address by the governor.

"Following this speech, I will not take any questions from the media. I will sign a proclamation tonight that will request all flags be flown at half staff to honor the fallen chief justice of the state supreme court. Our prayers, sympathies and sincere condolences go out to his family, friends and colleagues. A new chief justice will be appointed to temporarily fill the late chief justice's office."

The governor paused before continuing.

"The new chief justice is due to arrive here at any time tonight to begin his Senate confirmation hearing. This hearing is closed to the public due to the late hour of the hearing. The new chief justice was chosen by the outgoing chief justice as his preferred replacement. His name is Mr. Daniel S. Marcos."

Another pause while the cameras flashed and the video rolled for the evening news.

"The temporary appointment of Mr. Daniel S. Marcos, along with the emergency Senate confirmation hearing, was made possible by the speaker of the Senate who was prepared for this possible course of events. She was able to obtain a group of unbiased and voluntary Senators who took time away from their families and friends to be ready on a moment's notice to return here. To quote our former chief justice, 'Sometimes it becomes necessary to clean house on the bench'; that is all," said the governor as he stepped away from the podium and returned home.

Law enforcement personnel and the media finally caught up with Daniel at the restaurant. A large, muscular state trooper entered the private dining room. When he did, everyone put down their eating utensils and drinks to stare at him.

"Mr. Daniel S. Marcos!" he shouted.

Daniel stood up, wiping his mouth off with a napkin.

"Yes, Trooper, I am Mr. Daniel S. Marcos."

"Under the specific orders from the governor of the State of Colorado, I am to escort you immediately to the Capitol Building to the Senate chambers."

"For what purpose, trooper?" asked Daniel.

"To do a Senate confirmation hearing, Your Honor."

It suddenly hit Daniel what the trooper meant.

"May I take my family along?"

"Absolutely, Your Honor, and we will provide escort for your family and friends."

CHAPTER 12

Daniel made record time getting from the restaurant, which was in Lakewood, to the Capitol Building. The streets were lined, even at this late hour on a Friday night, with supporters and protestors. News reporters were camped out on the steps leading up to the front entrance. The Denver Police Department and the Colorado Highway Patrol were quick to clear a path for Daniel, his family, and his clients.

When they all entered the hallway and started walking up the spiral staircase towards the Senate chambers, cameras followed them. The party had microphones and questions thrown at them. Daniel politely, but firmly, replied, "No comment" while Todd and the others remained silent. When they finally made it to the entrance to the Senate chambers, the Sergeant-At-Arms stopped them.

"Wait right here, Mr. Marcos, while I announce you to the Speaker of the Senate," he said.

"Yes, sir."

The Sergeant-At-Arms looked over at the people standing behind and up against Daniel.

"Is this your family, Mr. Marcos?" he asked.

"Yes, sir."

The Sergeant-At-Arms showed them to the gallery observation room so they could see and hear Daniel on a one-way speaker and microphone combination. Seth had sent a quick text message to David while Chayton was running around wildly like all eight year olds do at important events. The Sergeant-At-Arms then showed the reporters where they could sit or stand to take pictures and shoot video footage for the early edition of the news. He then walked into the Senate chambers to speak to the Speaker of the Senate; she stood up and banged her gavel down several times for order.

"Attention in the Senate! Mr. Daniel Marcos has arrived."

The Senate chambers went from loud to quiet as the Sergeant-At-Arms led Daniel into the chambers. As Daniel stepped across the threshold onto the main floor, he could feel the power emanating from within. It was like a powerful aphrodisiac to him. Now he was beginning to understand why some people like the job of being a Senator.

The Sergeant-At-Arms ushered Daniel to a long, rectangular shaped table with a single chair for him. The chair was directly in front of a microphone and there was a small speaker to his left. When Daniel seated himself at the table, he saw a letter sitting in front of him, with his name on it. The Speaker of the Senate diverted his attention away from the letter.

"Good evening, Mr. Marcos; can you hear me all right?" asked the Speaker of the Senate.

"Yes, Madam Speaker, I can hear you just fine; can you hear me clearly?" asked Daniel, trying not to show his nervousness. The Speaker of the Senate and the other Senators could see it in his body language. They simply smiled at him knowing how nervous they felt when they first walked into the chambers.

"Before we begin, we would like to express our sincere condolences and sorrow over the recent and tragic loss of your friend, colleague and mentor."

"Thank you, Madam Speaker and thank you, Senators, for being here at such a late hour. I am sure that you have better things to do with yourselves on a Friday night than to be here," said Daniel, trying to choke back tears from the loss.

There was some chuckling from everyone at what Daniel had said.

"You're welcome, Mr. Marcos; this confirmation hearing is going to be informal. As you are probably aware, the deceased chief justice of the state Supreme Court named you as his preferred replacement until the November elections. He seemed not to trust either Associate Justices Hayes or Tartik."

"Yes, Madam Speaker, that is correct. He made that statement to me in open court in front of many witnesses. I can also understand his distrust of the two most senior associate justices."

"You're correct on those two points. In fact, your appeals case has earned it the highest viewer rating on Court TV since the Proposition 8 trial in 2010, as well as the most Internet views at over three million each. Now, let's get this hearing underway and we, as the Senate, would like to apologize for the late hour as well. I trust we didn't interrupt your dinner with your family?"

"No, Madam Speaker, I was finished with dessert when the welcoming committee arrived. Besides, it is very understandable, considering the circumstances."

Again, another round of chuckling, which made Daniel feel a little more relaxed, but he could still feel the power that surrounded him.

"The Senate appreciates your accommodations in return. Sergeant-At-Arms, would you please swear in Mr. Marcos?"

"Yes, Madam Speaker, with pleasure."

He walked over to Daniel who tried to conceal his nervousness. He raised his left hand and placed his right hand on the Holy Bible.

"Do you solemnly swear or affirm that the testimony that you're about to give is the truth, the whole truth and nothing but the truth?"

"I do."

"The Senate is now in session. The Senate recognizes Senator Mel Bonner of Senate District five; you have the floor for questioning," said the Speaker of the Senate.

"Thank you, Madam Speaker. Mr. Marcos, would you state, for the Senate records, your full name, place of residence and occupation?"

"Sure, Senator Bonner. My name is Daniel Santana Marcos. I live in Silverton and I am a criminal defense attorney currently practicing in Ironton, Colorado."

"Would that be the town of Silverton, Colorado, Mr. Marcos?" he asked.

"Yes, Senator Bonner, I apologize for not being specific enough."

"I know what you meant, but someone looking at these records decades from now might not draw the same conclusion. By the way, relax, you're among a great many friends and admirers of your work."

"Thank you, Senator Bonner."

"Do you possess the minimum qualifications of being the chief justice of the state supreme court?" asked Mel.

"Yes, except for one area and that is, I have never served as a judge or as a current or former associate justice of the state supreme court."

"Thank you for your honesty, Mr. Marcos. I will surmise that you are at least thirty-five years of age and have resided in the State of Colorado for at least fourteen years, either continuously or in aggregate total?"

"Yes, that is correct, Senator Bonner. I am fifty-two years of age and have resided in the State of Colorado since I turned thirty."

"Thank you, Mr. Marcos, I have no further questions."

The Speaker of the Senate saw Senator Robert Devins' left hand go up.

"Very well, the Senate now recognizes Senator Robert Devins of Senate District nine; you have the floor for questions," said the Speaker of the Senate.

"Thank you, Madam Speaker."

"Senator Devins, I hope that there are no hard feelings between us."

"None, Mr. Marcos. I made a big mistake and I paid the price for it. For what it is worth, it made me a better man and that is probably why I have served in my Senate district for the last six election cycles."

"I'm glad to hear that, sir."

"Mr. Marcos, what happens to a court case if the judge dies in open court, without closing the court properly and the court is still in session?"

"Generally speaking, another judge is brought in to finish the case. That judge, generally speaking, writes the opinions and conducts the sentencing hearings until a permanent judge is appointed, nominated or elected to the bench."

"At the level of the state supreme court, what happens then?"

"I am not familiar with the specifics of Article III of the Colorado Constitution as it deals with the death, disability, or incapacitation of the chief justice, or any of the associate justices while the court is in session."

"Thank you, Mr. Marcos. I have no further questions."

The Speaker of the Senate saw Senator Posh's right hand go up.

"Very well, the Senate now recognizes Senator Ikay Posh of Senate District seventeen; you have the floor for questions."

"Thank you, Madam Speaker. Mr. Marcos, did the deceased chief justice, prior to all that happened to you when you two shook hands, say court is adjourned, over, in recess until XYZ time, continued, postponed, etc.?"

"Not that I remember, Senator Posh."

"Did the deceased chief justice, at any time prior to all that happened when you two shook hands, bang down his gavel, kick a table leg, snap his fingers, knock on the tabletop, etc., in the courtroom?"

"Not that I remember, Senator Posh."

"Then, without either the chief justice, or one of the associate justices calling for a recess, etc., court is theoretically still in session, isn't it?"

"Generally speaking, yes, court is still in session."

"Can you vote in the decision or hear the rest of the appeals case as the interim chief justice?"

"Generally speaking, no, Senator Posh, it is an ethics violation of the oath of office for being a judge. However, since I had to be prepared for possible disbarment, I had turned over my private practice to my associate, Mr. Shilah Haynes. He can represent my clients in court if I am appointed as the newest chief justice of the state supreme court."

"Thank you, Mr. Marcos, I have no further questions."

The Speaker of the Senate saw Senator Jan Waters' left hand go up.

"Very well, the Senate now recognizes Senator Jan Waters of Senate District two; you have the floor for questions."

"Thank you, Madam Speaker. Before I ask my set of questions for you Mr. Marcos, would you please open up that letter in front of you?"

Daniel opened up the letter and read what had been written by the dying chief justice. The handwriting was very poor, and Daniel could tell it took a lot of strength for Chief Justice Wisenrock to have written the letter. He read it over twice before setting it back down on the tabletop.

"After having read the letter from the deceased chief justice, can you name any court cases where a deathbed confession has either been overturned or dismissed by the court, due to the person giving the deathbed confession's mental state of mind? This is in regards to the person's mental state of mind due to accident, injury or illness?"

"To the best of my knowledge, there has never been such a case. The chief justice's letter, combined with the fact that it was written in his own words by his own hands, meets the requirements of a deathbed confession. He knew, or probably knew, he was going to die."

"Thank you, I have no further questions."

The Speaker of the Senate waited for a few more minutes before speaking.

"Seeing no further hands going up for questions, the Senate will now conduct the confirmation vote electronically."

A few seconds went by before the number fifteen appeared in red on the large screen TV's in the chamber.

"Without further argument, this Senate hearing is hereby closed and the Senate can officially go home," said the Speaker of the Senate, banging down her gavel.

Everyone started celebrating on Capitol Hill that night. Daniel was rushed over to the Supreme Court for his swearing in ceremony. It had to be done that night so that Daniel, as the newly appointed chief justice of the Supreme Court, could close out the court's records properly.

Associate Justices Hayes and Tartik were flipping Daniel and the governor off along with mouthing foul words at the both of them. Daniel looked across the crowded courtroom and saw the clerk of the court standing there with the former chief justice's second set of robes. The press was there, Daniel's family was there along with his clients. As the governor was about to give the oath of office, David's face appeared on a small TV screen. The governor turned to face the associate justices.

"Normally, I have been told that the outgoing chief justice administers the oath of office to the incoming chief justice. Since that is not possible at this time, for obvious reasons, would one of you associate justices care to volunteer?"

Out of the ranks stepped Associate Justice Vince Kathryn.

"It would be my pleasure to swear in Mr. Marcos, governor."

"So be it," said the governor, stepping to one side while giving the Holy Bible and the oath of office speech to Associate Justice Kathryn.

Associate Justice Tartik stormed off to her chambers. The governor looked at Daniel, perplexed.

"Do you think you can handle Associate Justice Tartik there?" asked the governor.

"I'll certainly try, Governor."

Everyone started chuckling at Daniel's remark. The court Bailiff stood to Daniel's right. Daniel looked down at the TV screen to see and hear David speak.

"Congratulations Dad! I am very proud of you."

"Thank you, David, that means a lot to me right now."

"Mr. Marcos would you please put your left hand on the Bible and raise your right hand?"

"Yes."

Daniel repeated the action that he had just completed in the Senate chamber. Daniel could feel the power once again emanating from the courthouse and it started feeling good to him.

"I, state your full name," said Vince.

"I, Daniel Santana Marcos."

"Do solemnly swear by the Everliving God."

"Do solemnly swear by the Everliving God."

"That I will support the Constitutions of the United States and the State of Colorado."

"That I will support the Constitutions of the United States and the State of Colorado."

"And will faithfully perform the duties of the office of the Chief Justice of the supreme court of the State of Colorado upon which I am about to enter."

"And will faithfully perform the duties of the office of the Chief Justice of the supreme court of the State of Colorado upon which I am about to enter."

Daniel turned around to find the clerk of the court standing there with his robes and gavel.

"Your robes and your gavel, Your Honor."

"Thank you," said Daniel, putting the robes on and turning to face the governor to shake hands. Then they both turned to face the press.

"Ladies and gentlemen of the press and the citizens of the great State of Colorado, I present to you the newest chief justice of the state supreme court, Daniel Marcos. He is also the first and only Native American to hold this high an office within a state anywhere in the United States."

Court was convened immediately. Daniel, along with the other associate justices, even the two angry ones, assembled in the courtroom at 1:15 a.m. that Saturday morning.

"All rise, the Colorado State Supreme Court is now in session. The Honorable Chief Justice Daniel Marcos, presiding, over the appeals case of *Patricia Duffy-Downs Et. Al. v. The State of Colorado* case number 20AP7719."

They all sat down and Daniel looked out across a packed spectator's box, especially at this late hour of the night.

"You may be seated and this court will come to order. These proceedings are being recorded and broadcast as stated earlier. Since the final arguments were made, this court is adjourned until August 15th, 2021, when this court will start releasing its rulings and opinions," said Daniel, banging down the gavel one time.

"All rise," said the Bailiff as the justices all filed out of the courtroom.

Daniel's cell phone started buzzing at him, he looked down to see the text message that he had received: "The TITANIC has arrived in the Promised Land."

EPILOGUE

On September 30th, 2021, a much anticipated ruling on whether same-sex marriages should be legal, or not, came to a head. Thankfully, for Daniel, the former chief justice had written all of the opinions prior to his death. This made it easier for Daniel to conduct court business. The hatred flowing from Associate Justices Hayes and Tartik was never ending. Everyday was a fight with them on almost everything from when to recess for lunch to the opinions. The news was also waiting to record the outcome of the appeals case of *Patricia Duffy-Downs Et. Al. v. The State of Colorado*, case number 20AP7719. When the justices had all been seated, Daniel began his regular courtroom duties.

"You may be seated and this court will come to order. These proceedings are being recorded and broadcast at www.coloradocourtstv.gov\cssc\opinions\20AP7719.htm and on TV channels 505, 510 and 530. This opinion was written in full by the chief justice prior to his tragic death in this courtroom earlier this year."

Daniel suppressed any emotion before continuing.

"The opinion is a four to three vote with Associate Justices Robins, Hayes and Tartik dissenting. Associate Justices Kathryn, Smith, Hale and Chief Justice Marcos concur with the former chief justice's conclusions. The full opinion will be made available for downloading and review in sixty business days in accordance with court rules."

Daniel looked over at Associate Justices Tartik and Hayes before continuing.

"This court finds that both the trial court and the appellate court erred in the convictions of the plaintiffs in this appeals case. Therefore, the plaintiff's convictions are hereby overturned; it is so ordered. This court also finds that neither this court, nor any court in this state that is inferior to this court, has the right, privilege or authority to downgrade a same-sex marriage, civil union or whatever other legal definition is used by a governmental entity to identify a same-sex couple's committed relationship."

The courtroom erupted into cheers and boos all at the same time. Daniel banged down his gavel a few times before restoring order.

"This court finds that Colorado Revised Statutes, Title 15, Article 22, Part 112, known as the Designated Beneficiaries Agreement Act, provides no downgrading capability to any court of law in this state when the court is faced with such prospects as a same-sex couple that is either married, in a civil union, etc., as defined above. C.R.S. Title 15, Article 22, clearly, only provides for the UPGRADE of the Designated Beneficiaries Agreement to a full marriage."

There was stunned silence for a few minutes before Daniel continued.

"This court also finds that the State of Colorado has no reason to change the sexual orientation or sexual preference of any of the gays and lesbians living in the state or those that may come to this state to live. The State of Colorado also has no reason why it should limit the number of gays and lesbians in the state."

The cameras were rolling right along with the microphones.

"Further, this court finds nothing in either the wording or the intent of the legislature that the Designated Beneficiaries Agreement could be used to establish an intimate relationship for the purposes of meeting the two-prong test of the Domestic Violence Law, Colorado Revised Statutes, Title 18, Article 6, Part 800.3."

A lot of jaws dropped open on that statement.

"As for the other issues raised in the court over the validity of voter ballot initiative 45, titled the Colorado Defense of Marriage Act of 2006, this court finds that Article II, Section 31 of the Colorado Constitution violates Article II, Section 29 of the Colorado

Constitution and, therefore, makes Section 31 unconstitutional. Further, this court finds that, due to the lack of a paragraph D in Section 1 of Colorado Revised Statutes, Title 14, Article 2, Part 110, the legislature, whether on purpose or accidentally, created a protected class of citizens for certain crimes."

Many eyes in the courtroom opened wide on those words.

"This court further finds that Article II, Section 31, forces a number of Colorado State Government entities to have to discriminate against members of Colorado's LGBTQ community. This is in direct violation of Article II, Section 29 which provides that 'Equality of rights under the law shall not be denied or abridged by the state of Colorado or any of its political subdivisions on account of sex.' This court has ruled in six earlier rulings that the term 'sex' also extends to someone's actual or perceived sexual orientation or preference. One such governmental entity that is forced to discriminate against the LGBTQ community in the state is the Colorado Department of Public Health and the Environment."

Mr. Fargo looked at Daniel as if he had just lost all of his marbles.

"The Colorado Department of Public Health and the Environment is in charge of issuing and maintaining marriage licenses and certificates. Another governmental entity that gets away with discriminating against the LGBTQ community is the Colorado Child Adoption Agency with the requirement of fulfilling many parenting classes that are optional for opposite sex couples; it is so ordered."

Daniel waited before addressing the courtroom.

"Does the state wish to appeal this court's ruling?"

"Yes, Your Honor, and the State wishes to name you as the representative of the court in the civil action against invalidating provisions of the Colorado Constitution."

"I understand, Mr. Fargo. Do the plaintiffs wish to appeal this court's ruling?"

"No appeal, Your Honor, my clients and those similarly situated in this state would like to know when same-sex marriages may be legally performed and be legally valid and recognized in this state?" asked Shilah Haynes.

"Same-sex marriages cannot begin until the final disposition of this case by the U.S. Supreme Court, due to the state's request to appeal part of this court's decision."

"I understand, Your Honor and thank you for clarifying that matter."

"This court is adjourned," said Daniel, banging down his gavel.

"All rise," said the Bailiff.

Associate Justice Tartik walked up to Daniel and handed him two letters. Daniel looked at the letters of resignation which were to take effect immediately.

"Your letters of resignation are hereby accepted."

"You faggot loving bastard! I hope whatever deity you believe in will forgive you for your actions, because Associate Justice Hayes and I will never forgive you!" she said angrily.

"I understand; do you need any help in cleaning out your offices?"

"No, I think we can handle it ourselves," she said as she and former Associate Justice Hayes stormed off.

Daniel went to his chambers and called together the other associate justices to discuss names for possible replacement of the two associate justices that had left. Daniel came up with names, but each new name was crossed off almost as quickly until Daniel mentioned two names that all of the associate justices recognized and agreed with in principle.

"I thought that maybe former district appellate court judge for Division X, Donna Pinewood, would be a good replacement for Associate Justice Hayes," said Daniel. Daniel called her at her home number and she answered.

"Donna, it's Daniel; are you still looking for a job?"

"Yes, I am, and congratulations, Your Honor."

"Thank you and would you consider filling in for former Associate Justice Hayes' position on the bench?"

"Daniel, I would love to."

"Well, let me see if I can convince the governor to write-up a Temporary Appointment to the Bench Letter until the regular election cycle in 2014."

"Thank you, Daniel, for thinking of me; goodbye."

"One down, one to go, Daniel," said Associate Justice Smith.

"I hear you. Would anyone have any objections to former 10th Federal Circuit Court Judge Juliano Blatz?"

Daniel called him and he accepted as well.

With the case disposed of except for one part of it, the LGBTQ community was starting to plan on when same-sex marriages could begin. Daniel was able to win election for four years during the November election cycle. Daniel went through the same oath of office speech in front of cameras and the other justices and thought that all was in order. He had submitted his reasoning to the U.S. Supreme Court as to why the Colorado State Supreme Court had invalidated some of the state's constitutional amendments. On December 8th, 2021, Daniel received a phone call that he didn't think he would ever get. The clerk of the court for the Colorado State Supreme Court answered the phone.

"Hello?"

"Hello? Is Mr. Daniel Marcos at this number?" asked the voice.

"Yes, he is, but he is now Chief Justice Daniel Marcos of the Colorado State Supreme Court."

"Is he available, as the Chief Justice of the U.S. Supreme Court wishes to speak to him about some of his opinions and statements submitted with case number 21CV0915, *The State of Colorado v. The Colorado State Supreme Court Chief Justice Daniel Marcos Et. Al.*"

"One moment."

The clerk ran into Daniel's chambers and spoke to him. Daniel spoke to the Chief Justice of the U.S. Supreme Court for almost an hour before they hung up with each other. A few days later, the slip opinion was delivered to Daniel's personal email address instead of the court listed address for security reasons. He printed out the slip opinion and shared it with the other justices around Christmas time. He then called the people named in the case together for a special session of court.

"All rise, the Colorado State Supreme Court is now in session. The Honorable Chief Justice Daniel Marcos, presiding, over the case of *The State of Colorado v. The Colorado State Supreme Court, Chief Justice Daniel Marcos Et. Al.*, case number 21CV0915."

"You may be seated and this court will come to order. These proceedings are being recorded and broadcast at www. coloradocourtstv.gov\CSSC\21CV0915.htm as well as on TV channels 505, 515, 525 and 530. This court has received the final word from the U.S. Supreme Court in the case of *The State of Colorado v. The State of Colorado Supreme Court Chief Justice Daniel Marcos Et. Al.*, case number 21CV0915. This case has been assigned the official case number of 888 U.S. 1."

Daniel addressed the small crowd that had gathered. The crowd was small because severe weather in the Denver area had kept most people indoors and off the streets for safety reasons. Daniel, of course, knew that millions more were watching these proceedings on the Internet and on TV channels 505, 515, 525 and 530.

"The U.S. Supreme Court granted Writ of Certiorari to hear this case in accordance with Article III, Section 2 of the U.S. Constitution. However, due to time constraints and bad weather which would create an undue hardship on the parties in this case to come to Washington, D.C., this court carefully reviewed the arguments, statements and evidence presented by both sides in order to reach the following conclusions."

Daniel waited to see if anyone was taking notes before continuing.

"One, this Court, in a 9 to 0 vote, upholds the Colorado State Supreme Court's ruling of invalidating a certain provision of the state's constitution that was in direct conflict with another provision of the state's constitution. It is sometimes the job and necessary duty of the state supreme court to invalidate those amendments that conflict with each other. It is so ordered."

"Second, this Court upholds the second ruling in the case dealing with the powers of the state Supreme Court. It is so ordered."

Daniel looked over at the newest associate justices before continuing.

"This Court finds that Article II, Section 31, of the state's constitution known as the Defense of Marriage Act of 2006, also known as voter ballot initiative 45, forces a clear violation of Article II, Section 29 of the state's constitution upon the lesbian, gay, bisexual, transgendered and questioning, or LGBTQ, community by certain Colorado State Governmental Agencies such as the Colorado Department of Public Health and Environment, the Colorado Child Adoption Agency and other governmental run or controlled entities. It is true that the Colorado State Supreme Court has ruled six times in the past thirty years that the word 'sex' also refers to someone's sexual orientation or sexual preference actual or perceived. This is further evidenced by the state legislature adding to the Bias Motivated Crime statute, Title 18, Article 9, Part 121 of Colorado Revised Statutes to include 'someone's actual or perceived sexual orientation or preference.'"

There were gasps and outbursts which caused Daniel to have to stop reading the slip opinion and bang his gavel down several times to restore order.

"This Court, also in a 9 to 0 vote, holds that the Defense of Marriage Act of 2006, also known as voter ballot initiative 45, which became Article II, Section 31 of the state's constitution and its various ancillary wording in Titles 13 and 14 of Colorado Revised Statutes, violates Article I, Section 10 of the U.S. Constitution in three ways."

Daniel had to shuffle through some pages of bibliography before continuing.

"First, this Court has ruled that the voters of the fifty states, territories and protectorates, can, under the power given to them by the 9th Amendment to the U.S. Constitution, vote into place necessary, proper and reasonable laws. However, this court has had to rule a few times in its history that voters cannot pass laws that this court or any state supreme court or federal district court have struck down as being unconstitutional; i.e. miscegenation laws or sodomy laws, no matter what the reason given by the proponents of such a voter initiative. This court further finds this case is eerily similar to *Romer V. Evans*, 517 U.S. 620, 1996."

Daniel looked at the small crowd once again before continuing.

"Second, this Court finds that the voters also cannot pass laws which unfairly restrict, limit or prohibit contracts. This court has ruled no less than fifteen times in its history that a marriage is considered a contract between two people. When the Colorado legislature in 2018 passed Senate bill SB18-0900 which became law on July 1, 2018, breach of contract became a criminal only offense. Therefore, we find that within the wording of Article I, Section 10 of the U.S. Constitution of 'no state shall make any laws that impair the obligation of a contract' applies to Article II, Section 31 of the Colorado Constitution. Article II, Section 31 clearly falls into that category and is therefore unconstitutional. The voters do not have the power to do something that is forbidden to the legislature whether this is at the federal level or the state level via the voter ballot initiative process."

Daniel had to turn a few more pages before continuing.

"This Court further finds that Colorado Revised Statutes, Title 14, Article 2, Part 104, Section 3, paragraph B, being that breach of contract in the state is considered a criminal only offense currently, falls within the purview of the ex post facto law test of Article I, Section 10 of the U.S. Constitution. This is clearly another area that is off limits to the voters."

People in the courtroom were all wide awake at this point.

"This Court will not even entertain the violations of Article IV, Section 1 of the U.S. Constitution as that is self-evident by the wording of Article II, Section 31 of the state constitution. As for the law being a violation of the 5th Amendment's protection against self-incrimination in a court of law, except as provided for during a grand jury investigation, the court finds it does violate the 5th Amendment's privilege of no self-incrimination on the witness stand. But, this law in question goes one step further by not validating or recognizing same-sex unions (marriage, civil unions, etc.); one spouse would have to bear witness against the other one in a court of law. This court has almost always upheld the husband/wife marriage immunity privilege, etc., in a court of law except for certain felony level crimes."

There was almost total rebellion on those words.

"Order!, Order! Order in my courtroom!" yelled Daniel, banging his gavel down repeatedly to restore order.

"This Court also finds that the Colorado Defense of Marriage Act of 2006 Et. al. violates the 14th Amendment's two clauses of equal protection; i.e. 'No State shall make or enforce any law which shall abridge the privileges or immunities of citizens of the United States nor shall any state deny to any person within its jurisdiction the equal protection of the laws.' It is the ruling of this Court that in upholding the correct interpretation of the Colorado State Supreme Court, Article II, Section 31 and all of its ancillary wording in Colorado Revised Statutes shall be stricken from the state's constitution. This ruling will apply to the other states that have passed similar measures so as to prevent further civil suits from clogging up the court system. It is so ordered; signed Chief Justice Joanne L. Snyder, United States Supreme Court."

Daniel looked up at the crowd who was now waiting to hear some very much, long awaited news.

"Your Honor, when can same-sex marriages begin?" asked Shilah on behalf of Daniel's former clients.

"Same-sex marriages can begin starting July 1, 2023 so as to give the legislature and other state governmental agencies time to do all the necessary and proper administrative tasks"

"Your Honor, when are same-sex marriages, civil unions, etc., going to be recognized and valid?" asked Shilah.

"This court rules that any same-sex marriage, civil union, etc., is valid and recognized immediately; this court is adjourned," said Daniel, standing up and banging down his gavel.

"All rise," said the Bailiff.

When they were behind closed doors, the Speaker of the Senate arrived to speak to Daniel. The clerk of the court brought the speaker into Daniel's chambers where she handed Daniel a blue colored envelope.

"What is in there, Madam Speaker?" asked Daniel, almost afraid to find out.

"The names of the four Senators and one Representative that wish to go through the impeachment process."

"I understand and I will be ready in March if that will be enough time?"

"The third week of March would be the best time, Your Honor."

"So be it."

After she left, Daniel asked for two other associate justices to assist him with the impeachment hearings. The two youngest associate justices volunteered to assist him. Monday, March 20th, 2022, arrived all too soon for Daniel and the other justices. They walked across the streets with their robes tucked under their arms.

When they had cleared security, they put their robes on and walked up to the entrance to the Senate chamber. The Speaker of the Senate banged her gavel down several times.

"Attention in the Senate! All rise for the Chief Justice of the Colorado State Supreme Court Daniel Marcos, Associate Justice Vince Kathryn and Associate Justice Bianca Hale."

Daniel and the other justices were shown where to sit by the Sergeant-At-Arms for the Senate. Daniel sat down and banged his gavel once.

"You may be seated and this court will come to order. My associate justices and I are here to conduct impeachment trials in accordance with the Colorado State Constitution's provisions for such in both Article I and Article III."